LS6

DEADINK

LS6

by
Mario Crespo

Translated by
Sally Ashton with Steve Dearden

DEADINK

DEADINK

First published in Great Britain in 2016 by Dead Ink
An imprint of Cinder House Publishing Ltd.

ISBN 978-0-9934014-0-4

Translated by Sally Ashton

Cover art by Russtle

Printed and bound by CPI Group (UK) Ltd, Croydon,
CR0 4YY

WWW.DEADINKBOOKS.COM

To Mirian.

LSI

151

1.

'What's your favourite day of the year?'

I hate a girl asking me existential questions when I don't even have her phone number. It has just gone eight in the morning and I am lying next to Amanda. Amanda Amanda Amanda; at least her name turns me on. I get up, open the curtains and light rushes in like a crowd when the sales open at one of those big department stores. My image of her blonde hair hanging over me fades. For a Spaniard, getting laid in England means nothing. Once it's late enough you can just sign out any girl who's up for it. I don't find English girls that attractive anyway, but this one's a real dog. The whisky is pretty rough too. Though I like the way it cuts through inhibitions.

Valladolid, Burgos, Pamplona, Logroño, León. My dad took years to choose a place to settle. During my adolescence in eighties Northern Spain there was none of the post-Franco letting go like they had in Madrid, nor the Ibiza sex party, so getting laid wasn't easy. I should have come to this island years ago. What's your favourite day of the year? Please girl, no. Don't ask me these things.

2.

The history of Great Britain is a list of great names; Shakespeare, Churchill, Lennon. Centuries of history have been ruled from this little island, and that would have been quite a trick to pull off without committing excesses. But, for me, there are two key moments in the history of Great Britain: the Industrial Revolution and the madness of Margaret Thatcher. And, apart from the Irish problem, unlike in Latin countries, there have been no internal ideological wars, just the cold Labour party machine or the Tories' naked greed to ensure the place functions economically. The calm this brings creates the perfect environment to develop The Plan – the perfect place to establish economic liberalism. In fact, whatever kind of liberalism you fancy. But there is something else that makes this island a magnet. I don't know if I can explain it in words, it's a kind of energy that emanates from the people, from this atmosphere so enveloping that it makes you… think.

Up all night with an ice-cold glass in my hand. Another one, please. I imagine Thatcher excited, on the attack, wetting her lips with Johnnie Walker Black Label, watching her ultraliberal ideas take over the civilised world. The regulators collapsing, the value of money undermined – and our savings. In Paris I paid six Euros for a tiny beer. How much would I have paid for a BMW? Thatcher and Reagan said that the state was not the solution, but the problem, so they let the market into our pants and advertising did the rest. Later we just ripped our knickers off for them. They turned us into perfect consumers who would pay triple what a flat was worth. Now, twenty-five years later, states are injecting taxpayers' money into the financial system, and Thatcher's knelt, arse in the air, knickers round her ankles.

The Industrial Revolution, the abandonment of the colonies, the opening up of Europe's borders. The waves of migration driven by the continual demand for cheap manual labour. Pakistanis, Indians, West Indians, Africans, Poles. The cosmopolitan nature of this country fascinates me. This is what it is to live in the world. A Tower of Babel without stairs. I didn't know much about England before coming here – of Wales, Scotland and Ireland I still know nothing – and the only thing that I knew about Leeds was that it had a football ground called Elland Road. Football is culture. I landed in London to learn English and months later decided that Leeds was its equal. Well, similar, but cheaper. A kind of subsidiary but the capital of Yorkshire. Proud of its roots. It's not easy to understand their accent or their dialect, but here I have always felt at home.

3.

I am bored by casual fucks. I've forgotten how I used to chat up Spanish girls. I'm brusque, cold, dry, like a Viking in a brothel. I lack feeling, the great overwhelming, eyeball to eyeball, simultaneous orgasm. Looking at the sleeping face of this troll Amanda, I decide to masturbate more often. I need the chase, to play more – to be flattered, I need to believe that somebody likes me. It's no longer enough to know that at 5 AM I can pull the first girl who's up for it, or takes off her top in a club, the first mediocre pub blonde that offers to buy me a drink.

With my pants falling down and trainers in hand, I whisper goodbye to Amanda. Saying her name gives me a pleasure that she couldn't give me herself. I stumble down the stairs, turn into what appears to be the lounge and leave the house by the back door. Hers is the last terrace. Some trees and then the ring road. Her street is un-tar-macked and I have to step through puddles before I am on the road where I can stop a passing taxi. I am in Leeds 6, LS6, near the rugby ground and not far from my house.

Back in Leon I learnt my trade in one of the state-run Parador hotels, then went freelance. I have served at a Socialist Worker Party meeting, at dinner with Real Madrid, at the country estate of Enrique Ponce, Victori-no's farm, sliced for Fabio Capello, wielded my knife for ministers, ambassadors, from regional mayors to the hus-band of the Infanta. One day I smashed some guy's face in. I was tired of it all. It really bothers me when people laugh at my profession. I count to ten, breathe deeply and try to picture rolling waves, but sometimes I just can't contain myself. I'm a cutter. I cut ham.

As a freelancer I earned good money, but then came hard times, when only the strong survive. Someone suggested England. Yeh man, it's an experience and you can learn English, earn loads of cash. It was this good socio-eco-nomic advice that led me to this island. And, since then, I'm just one more who misses driving on the right, the Mediterranean sun and eating suckling pig – but it doesn't matter, I became a product of the red bricks, always saying thank you and smiling even when I want to kill the guy I'm talking to. Here, democracy is in the bloodstream and living easier than in Spain. Everything is easier. The crisis is the only thing that worries me. Until now, I have not had much luck. I have been in England five years now and still I have not brandished the carving knife, still not cut the ham.

In 2009 consumer spending plummeted. The people of Leeds don't go out to eat out as much as they did before, only to drink. Little by little they've reduced their living costs. As a waiter I see everything. A waiter needs to use a little psychology – manipulate customers. As a waiter I can do a social study on any aspect of life based on the customers that we serve on a Saturday night. So I saw the slump coming, how my manager's takings fell, then the reduction in our hours and, finally, I am a waiter no more. They've had to let me go.

4.

The taxi drops me on The Headrow across from the library. I nip into a newsagent and buy Lucozade and a Lion Bar. Soon after arriving here I'd discovered that this cheap breakfast gave me enough energy to search for work for four hours at a time. I've been unemployed for a week and am bored. But with this economy it is not going to be easy to get a job.

I cross The Headrow, the city's main drag, and walk quickly up Park Row, trying to put as much distance between me and my old workplace as possible. I don't fancy bumping into any of my ex-workmates, picking at that old scab, because the goodbye ended up being pretty unpleasant. Just as I am about to turn down Bond Street, a huge guy grabs my arm.

'Carlos! Fuck me!' I say.

He's a chef, he came over from Angola with all his family. A freak of nature with a big heart. His whole family are in work, but according to Carlos they still spend too much. He does all the hours he can in the kitchen, then spends the rest of the day on the street looking for daytime work.

'You doing good bro?'

'Yeh man, all good, how goes it with you?'

'Did you know the manager is shagging Neli the Colombian?'

'Really? Yes?'

Neli. Fuck. I'd like to be in the manager's shoes. I can't pull the Latinas anymore. I tell Carlos I am in a rush, he looks at me oddly and smiles, and I dash away from my past.

Bond Street is one of the pedestrian streets in the centre of Leeds. I don't know what was here before the mid-20th century, but nowadays it is an enormous commercial playground, a perfect grid of wide streets, all pedestrianised, all linked by the famous Arcades. Dozens of entrances and exits add to the confusion. Victorian architecture, you either love it or hate it. Streets rammed, people bump you at every step, legs moving like automata, carrying branded bags of clothes, trainers, mobile phones. People from Bradford, York and the whole of Yorkshire come to shop in this commercial enclave in the heart of England.

At the end of Albion Street, where the shops peter out, is the employment office, the Job Centre. I need to sort out my benefits as soon as possible. It must be after nine-thirty

– my body is begging me for coffee. So, on my way, I nip into Waterstones and have a cappuccino while scanning the sports pages. Liverpool v Chelsea in the quarter finals of the Champions League.

5.

In the Job Centre I sit in one of the few free seats next to an old lady with grey hair. She seems nervous, agitated. I know that any moment now she will think up some banal comment or meaningless question just to start a conversation. She drums her fingers on her thigh, glancing at me. I know she wants to talk, she looks like a loner, but I'd prefer things to stay like this, in silence, until my number's called.

'Young man, do you know about the Speenhamland system?' she says.

'No.'

'Difficult to pronounce, isn't it?'

'Yep, sure is.'

'It's a grant created in 1795 for poor country people who, even though they were working, couldn't make enough to live on.'

'Mrs, I don't even have a job.'

'You know, young man, the Speenhamland scheme is another of this country's con-tricks. It's because they give these hand-outs that we have so many spongers, you know, and why pay is so low.'

I don't know how much more I can take of this old dear. She's making me nervous with her views on the world. I love economics, I read the financial papers and dream of having my own business, but I'm not in the mood to talk. My number comes up on the little screen. I'm lucky; last time they kept me waiting over half an hour. As I reach the door I bang into a girl who snarls that it's her turn. Pink tracksuit, massive gold hoops, florescent trainers, matching baseball cap – a scally, a chav, or, as we'd say in Spanish, a choni.

'You alright, love?' says a lanky ginger bloke holding a child.

'This twat says he has my number.'

Ginger leaves the kid on the seat and strides over, asks me please for my number.

'66,' I say, showing it him.

His chica also has 66. She shows it me, looking sideways at the kid. Ginger slaps the side of my head, my vision blurs, I double up. He waves his enormous hand centimetres from my face. Gives me another slap. He chucks the paper on the floor and, as it falls, I see that my ticket is not 66, it's 99.

There are five desks to deal with 33 numbers. Twenty minutes to wait. The only empty seat left is next to the old dear. I decide to go out for a smoke. In the street I bump into Jesus, from Oviedo, another who worked in the restaurant. He used to make a killing on the side selling pirated movies and CDs, but now he only deals in really illicit stuff. He tells me that, as I'm unemployed, I should leave where I'm living and move in to the place he is squatting, which is legal in England. He offers me a fag, says to call him later so he can show me the room. We puff away in silence. I smoke right down to the filter, thinking how this isn't a great time to be paying rent. I tell Jesus to hang on. I ring my landlady and tell her I don't want the room any more. She says I have a week to pack my stuff and collect my deposit. She messes up my head. I hate her; I fancy her. I have always liked older women – she goes to Spain a lot and understands our culture. She would need proper work, proper chatting up – that's why I like her and that's why she's out of my league.

Jesus and I shake on it and he agrees to meet me at the squat in an hour.

6.

Back in the waiting room the old lady has gone. They're on number 101. I try to get in front of the guy who is up next, but see that I'll end up getting slapped like before. Not a scally this time, but his creased forehead and scarred face tell me he is a hard type, not someone you'd want as your enemy. I let him pass and leave the Job Centre, having sorted nothing.

For me, England has always meant football, rugby, hooligans. For me, England was Bobby Charlton, Paul Gascoigne, Manchester United. Far away dreams that I only knew from TV, but they were big things for me, important. Knowing where you fit in is not always easy.

The trick is to know at the time, otherwise you'll spend your life wanting to return to a station the train has already left. A few months ago I realised I fitted in here. My destiny. I have a theory about us Spaniards who decide to settle in England; we are weirdos, introverts, wanting to start from scratch, escaping something we can't describe. We don't miss the sun or the food. I love this country, even the bad stuff.

There are days when all the shit arrives at once. You just have to deal with it. Maybe finding work is more of a priority than sorting out where to live, but I leave the Job Centre and make for the squat. I want to see the room, close the deal with Jesus and start to move my things in. It begins to rain and, without me really knowing why, the title of a film floats into my head, Aguirre, the Wrath of God. I've never seen it, but I like the comma, the comma after Aguirre. Who was this Aguirre? I associate the title with the poster, it makes me think of The Mission. I see myself as Jeremy Irons, conquering a new world.

I leg it to Woodhouse Lane, through all the puddles, crazy because I'm wearing Munich trainers that cost me over a hundred quid. It must be eleven by now, but I am not sure because the battery's gone on my mobile. What a day. Not a soul in the street. Not that I would see them if they were, everything is so grey...

Hyde Park is... well, a little park. Compared with Spain, we should really call it a big park. A typical bit of English greenery, an open natural space, no concrete, no swings. In this country, the tiniest glimpse of sun and people flood out – suddenly the grass is covered with Anglo-Saxon pink, the sky fills with barbecue smoke, the smell of cheap hot dogs, the great outdoors, dope.

The park runs along the side of the Leeds University. This is the student area. A little further along, by the Grand Mosque, is the Pakistani area, the air full of spices.

I arrive at Hyde Park soaked, cut across and go down one of the side streets and then, a few metres ahead, see the squat. It's an old student house. Both the gate and the door are open. There's no bell and I'd feel a dickhead shouting, so I go in. A barking dog and the stench of marijuana guide me down the hall. In the lounge a ginger Rasta lies across one of the sofas. I guess Jesus' room must be upstairs. I turn and am surprised by him right behind me. He gives me a creepy little smile I'm not sure how to interpret. We go up and he shows me the room. There's just a bed and a wardrobe.

Out of nowhere, he asks, 'Do you believe in freedom?'

'In freedom? Sure, of course, what are you on about?'

'We're into freedom here. We're not tied down by any-body else's shit, OK? We're for truth, free thought, doing whatever we like, experimenting with everything.'

'Yeh yeh, that's OK in theory, mate, but you try getting a job without taking someone else's shit – the only way to be free in this place would be to become a hermit. Where's the bathroom?'

'I work the system when it suits me. Like, instead of letting it fuck with me, I fuck with it. If you understand that, life is simple: no National Insurance Number, no ID, no driver's license, no council tax, no rent. Like I'm saying, we live outside the system, but if there's a grant going, there's no problem getting false papers. This is the best country in the world. It's all there for the taking, no need to be hermits. But hey, guapo, I am talking about another kind of freedom.'

'What?'

'Sexual.'

'Oh yeh,' I say. 'Now that is what I do like about this country. I've fucked here like I've never fucked before.'

'And have you experimented, no?'

'I've done a lot of dirty stuff.'

'Would you like to make love with me?'

'What?'

'Yes, here, would you like to try it?'

'Yes, sure, fine… but you said we all do whatever we like, yes? You see… that's not really my… the answer is no. No way am I shagging you.'

'OK. Feel at home. The door is always open. Bring your stuff whenever you want.'

7.

I leg it from the old student house and head straight home, feeling like a small boy hazed for the first time. Stupid, weak, vulnerable. No. I didn't fancy being bedded by a bloke one bit, let alone him.

Zig-zagging through the warren of the red brick Pakistani area, I arrive at Headingley Stadium, one of the most hallowed bits of turf in England. Two stadiums in one – rugby and cricket. I worked here for a bit as a waiter. Seeing the buildings gives me a lift. Sport gives me a purpose, plugs me back into reality – the league tables, the stats. In the squat I felt asphyxiated, but now, dwarfed by the huge seating stands, I begin to enjoy my walk home.

I get there, make straight for the fridge. Nothing. As I can't eat, I pack my bags. A doubt forms in my head. Flashing images, like crime scene shots, which are gone as quickly as they come. Leaving my bags, I nip to the parallel street and, without knocking, enter my landlady's office. I see nothing but her pencil skirt. I already have a hard-on and a smirk, a smirk of relief as I feel the testosterone kick in. No doubts there. She looks great. Short skirt and high boots. She turns and I can't look her in the eyes, because of the way her top's cut, her tits, she looks at me like what am I doing there. That's when I know I am not going to live in the squat, because kissing the back of necks is my thing, not biting pillows. I am in love with this British woman with Spanish blood and need to fuck her. I don't know if this is a real feeling or just an illusion from my being so low. Whatever. She has given me the motivation to resume cutting ham.

'I changed my mind, I decided to stay, Lisa.'

'It's me who decides what happens here. Like I said earlier, you have a week to get out.'

And she means it. I have a week to sort out the mess that is my room so I can get back all of my deposit. A week to find enough of a job to allow me to pay a month's rent in advance somewhere. A week to sell off some of my belongings cheap, to make a new start, to cut something other than ham. Thinking about all this makes me anxious, stressed, numb. The best thing would be a day away from all this, to relax. Nino is the solution.

Nino drives a red Ford Focus decorated Hindi style, but has a broad Leeds accent. A third generation Indian who deals in weed, pills and cocaine. I only need a little weed. I'd prefer hash, but it's not what they smoke here. Perhaps it is only a Spanish thing, because we have easy access to cheap home-grown, but I am not used to the highs of this genetically modified shit packed with THC. It's too strong for me. But my ears are still ringing from the ginger hooligan's smack, and being humiliated by his scally with the gold hoops, the suffocation of the squat and being chucked out of my flat. I'm low. I need a smoke. I need Nino.

He tells me he will be with me in a couple of hours. Bastard. I slump on the sofa, switch on the TV, begin watching a film called This Is England, but fall asleep. They don't take siestas in England, that's why they are always knackered.

I'm woken by the phone. It takes a few seconds to remember where I am. Nino tells me he will be in the usual place in a couple of minutes. I've been asleep for ages.

Nino arrives at the gate of the stadium at 17.58. Two minutes early. I told you he was British. I get in the car and give him a twenty. As always, the merchandise is under the handbrake. As always, I wait until we are at the traffic lights before I discreetly pocket it. The M.O. is always the same, once round the block and back to where we started. We never say much, just talk about the strength of the gear or other stuff he can sell me.

The traffic lights go to amber, then green. You get amber both ways with the Saxons. We jump the green, by hundredths of a second. The Recaro racing seat absorbs my body mass. By the time the other cars are off, the Hindi Ford Focus is a hundred metres down the road. First –

second – third. An explosion of air and gasoline, pistons in my head. We fly through Headingley, the exhausts rasping. Nino is off his head. Angry, tense, aggressive. I have never seen anyone drive so violently. 5600 rpm in third. He spins the wheel right. The tires screech. The car slides and shudders but Nino fights the g-force and straightens. I nearly piss myself, but also feel alive; this is better than my dull boring life. I am enjoying this and for a second I think, Why not? Why not die now?

The woman backing out must be thinking the same thing. If only Nino was driving at normal speed, he would have time to brake, but Nino is in a rally...

The last thing I see is his body flying, going through the windscreen like a ball from a canon. The fatal arc of no seat belt. The impact is spectacular. We'd hit the bend with no time to react. The red Focus inside the yellow Beatle, fucking it up the arse.

When I come round someone is trying to get me out of the car. A voice says, Don't move him! My nose is pouring blood, but there's no pain. To my left, through the smashed windscreen, I can see Nino outside on the road. He waves, Come on, get out! The same guy who tried before helps me out of the mash of red metal my Hindi dealer's motor has become. He and his wife must have seen the crash. I get them to look to the woman in the other car and stumble over to Nino who is up, limping badly and bleeding from his head. Then I see the speed limit, 30 mph.

'We have to get out of here,' he says. 'Disappear. I'm carrying all this gear, and a weapon. Move your arse!' he slurs.

I'm scared shitless. I have enough problems without

the police on my back. Nino jumps the fence of an old people's home and disappears into their huge garden. He has balls, this guy. He looked much more injured than me. The couple are trying to find the pulse of the woman in the Beatle. The bloke says, 'She's dead!' The woman runs off for help while he calls an ambulance on his mobile. I go back and open the passenger door of the VW and see what's what. I grab the handbag lying on the seat. The bloke clocks me but is too busy answering the 999 guy's questions. He looks nervous, walks away towards the main road. Time to get out of here. I jump the old people's gate and lose myself in the trees.

8.

Crouching in the undergrowth, I hear the first sirens. With darkness falling they won't be able to see me. There's no sign of Nino. He must be more used to this kind of fuck up than me. I've never been an angel, but this is too much. I want to help the woman, but don't know what to do. I can't think straight, my body aches. I have to sit down. I feel the pain that my fear cancelled out before. The amount of blood on my hands scares me. Running around like a dickhead isn't going to help, I need to think.

'Are you alright, lad?'

I look up and there's the silhouette of a little hunch-backed bloke.

'Are you OK, lad?'

'Yes, no, no worries, I fell.'

'You work here?'

'Oh, no, no, yeh… I'm a salesman. I came here to sell some stuff and couldn't find my way out.'

The man takes a couple of steps towards me and squats.

'You're bleeding, lad. Come with me to our medical room. We'll sort you out.'

Going to A&E might give me away, so I agree to go with the old guy. He is kind, helps me get up, and walks me down a path lined with little cypress trees. The place is pretty gloomy, but him being there makes me feel OK.

'You're a salesman, eh? Must be hard work. All this neo-whatever only works when times are good. So now what? Why don't we just get rid of all the teachers and doctors?'

'Mm, they're essential,' I say through the blood in my nose.

'No, young man, the only essential is money. No money, people don't spend, so you don't have salaries for all the doctors. Obvious, isn't it?'

'Doctors'll always be in demand,' I say, as if I always have conversations like this when I'm bleeding from the nose.

'Ah, but it's not economics – a patient isn't buying a product, they just want to survive. That's why it doesn't make sense saying the state is the problem. You understand, lad?'

Out of the haze of orange street lamps a three-storey building appears. The old guy is beginning to remind me of the woman from this morning. But at least he is doing something useful. He asks me to use the doormat and I can see why, the mud off my shoes wipes out the W and E of WELCOME.

'Hello John, love,' says a voice coming from the corner, a nurse sat behind a counter smiling at us.

'Hello Linda,' replies the old guy, stopping. I'm skulking right behind him to avoid her looking too closely, but John grasses me up. 'I met this salesman in the park, he's fallen and bloodied his nose,' he tells the nurse.

She says, 'Then go on in, Lilly's still there.'

A white light silhouettes Lilly the doctor. My swollen eyes have reduced my vision to cinemascope and I can just about see her turn as she hears us enter. The scene reminds me of Kim Novak in Vertigo, I am not sure if her face is illuminated or if it is the source of the light.

She smiles hesitantly before asking, 'What happened, John?'

He explains and as he turns to leave, nods to me, 'A pleasure.'

The Doc says, 'So, you're a salesman...'

'Yes.' I clear my throat.

'So what do you sell then? Knives?'

'No, no, I sell…. um, office furniture.'

'I didn't think any salesmen had been in today.'

'Yeh… I was with the manager.'

'It's odd for a salesman to have cuts on his fingers like these.'

'Ah, yes, an accident, at home. My girlfriend had a bad shoulder so couldn't cut the ham.'

'So you're Spanish. I was thinking you were either Spanish or Italian.'

'Yes, yes, I like to cut ham.'

'They say it's an art. My father organises VIP events, sometimes they get professional ham carvers in all the way from Spain.'

'All the way… from Spain?!'

'Yes, we don't have many round here,' she laughs.

'No way, it can't be.'

'You don't believe me?'

'Listen, Lilly, you're Lilly right?'

'Doctor Lilly.'

'Then Doctor, listen, this is really, really important for me, I can cut ham like a professional. What? Shit, I am a professional! Tell your dad, if he needs a professional ham cutter he should call me. I want to change jobs. I am bored of selling chairs. You'll do it?'

'You're weird. A bit of a dark horse. I don't know how you got your broken nose, but I like your style. And you do seem more excited by ham than office chairs.'

'You'll do it?'

'Sure, leave me your name and number, Mr… ?'

'Alvarez, Francisco José Alvarez.'

'Muy bien Señor Alvarez, now tip your head back.'

By the time I get out, everything is black, everything silent. Still no trace of Nino. My field of vision has reduced even more. My eyelids are heavy, my cheeks swollen, two tennis balls below my eyes. Lilly bandaged up my nose so I have to breathe through my mouth. But that's nothing, a small price in exchange for the chance of work with her dad. I've had a crap day, full of crap things happening, crap feelings. Hard shit. One of those days that ends with you deciding to sort your life out. But at least today there's been something – a golden ticket, the opportunity to get on with my life.

Before heading home – my home for a little longer, at least – I nip back to the bushes where I hid the Beatle woman's bag. I take everything that might be useful: eighty quid, a packet of tobacco and two tickets for the theatre, then beat it.

Two theatre tickets. What if I invited my landlady to the play? She likes drama and the tickets are for VIP seats, which might make her like this trendy middle class Spaniard after all.

It starts soon. I'll ring her. But, thinking about it, I know it's a useless idea, she'll be out having a meal with one of her boyfriends. I chuck one of the tickets away and disappear.

LS2

1.

Whenever she was in her 'zero-space,' Julianne Redgrave asked herself, what is the point of being a seventy year old woman all alone in the world?

Zero-space was what Julianne called those passive moments when her mind began to think all by itself. Moments when she did not want to read a novel, or watch the telly, or go for a walk. Raw moments, uncomfortable.

A human being is defined by what they do with whatever freedom they manage to achieve for themselves. Julianne had achieved very little in her seven decades and had been frustrated by her lack of freedom, her inability to go off the beaten path, to improvise – she felt a kind of cowardice, resignation, defeat. Julianne had been taught that, in an ideal life, a woman, like a minor goddess, needed spoiling and kindness, needed to feel protected, needed the security of a man in exchange for doses of carnal and emotional satisfaction. This is what she was expecting. And for a while she believed it: losing her virginity, getting married, having children. Another world. Julianne could not remember if she was happy then, though they were the only memories she still clung to from the time before real life appeared and spat, Hello, here I am, see how I treat you and no matter what, you are going to have to put up with me. That was when she realised that you can't go back in time in a DeLorean, that there was a moment you had to do certain things, that you had to adapt before it was too late. Sometimes she even wished her husband was still alive.

In 1983 Julianne found out that she didn't need her husband any more. Great Britain was at war with Argentina. The Malvinas for some, the Falklands for others, or the Fucklands for those who were more critical. Thatcher, the recapture of the islands, huge strikes, riots, immigration, the dole. England was going through one of the most turbulent times in its history, a period of change the long-term consequences of which were unknown. Julianne was one of the first people to find out. Her husband, a sergeant in the army, was killed. Her eldest son rebelled against the martial law that his father imposed and become a yob, a teenage hooligan ready to confront the world. Her youngest was diagnosed with autism. Julianne was used to running the house, but not to making decisions. At first, the situation overwhelmed her. Then, four years after her husband died, her sons left for London. The older to work, the younger to study. Neither returned to live in Leeds.

Spring arrived with no light, but Julianne woke up with a new energy. Well rested. At night, she occupied her zero space, alone with her thoughts. She slept soundly. Not thinking about herself, but about society, the system. When you reach a certain age, you confront things that seemed to be problems and laugh at all the time you wasted worrying about them. You don't have to give in to grey hairs, you can still have dignity, style – be as chic as you were at thirty. But the crumbling body is not easy to accept. Julianne had an appointment with her hairdresser first thing – Marisa a Cape Verdean, who backcombed her hair like a Hollywood star. She felt pampered, valued. She might not know what she would do with the rest of her life, but she knew she wanted to love it and she did not want to lose any more time.

2.

To make the most of the time you have here, you have to learn to let go. Julianne didn't have much to do and, not having much money, monotony was her worst enemy. She would have liked to travel to see Cornwall, Kent, Wales. She would have liked to visit her sons more often, wander down Oxford Street, sit and watch the world go by in Piccadilly, dine in a fancy restaurant overlooking the Thames. But she couldn't even afford the bus fare down there. Fridays she drank coffee with other widows, her subsidised friends, other representatives of frustration, each time duller than the last. But solitude was worse than tedium.

While Julianne was friendly and would chat to anyone standing next to her at the bus stop, in the supermarket queue or the newsagents, Marisa was a real chatterbox. A skilled hairdresser, technically and psychologically. She had a British passport but was proud of her roots. She talked about the Orishas, of African rites, of unearthing the energy inside us. Julianne was fascinated. She hung on every word.

'You are so beautiful, Julianne,' said Marisa.

'I'm too old for flattery, my dear. After forty you're invisible to men.'

'You go out there, walk down the street, then come back and tell me that.'

Julianne sighed, 'I don't wander the street much these days, though today I've to go and sort out my pension. There's so many unemployed these days they keep you waiting for hours.'

'Wait, I'll come with you.'

Julianne looked at Marisa, surprised.

'Cos I need a fag,' said the hairdresser, holding up her packet.

In the Job Centre waiting room a young Spanish looking man sat beside her. Young people might know all about technology, fashion, modern music, the internet, but know nothing of the daily traps the system lays in their way.

'Young man, do you know about the Speenhamland system?' she says.

'No.'

'Difficult to pronounce, isn't it?'

'Yep, sure is.'

'It's a grant created in 1795 for poor country people who, even though they were working, couldn't make enough to live on.'

'Mrs, I don't even have a job.'

'You know, young man, the Speenhamland scheme is another of this country's con-tricks. It's because they give these handouts that we have so many spongers, you know, and why pay is so low.'

He didn't seem very friendly for a Mediterranean type, then he tried to jump the queue in front of a pair of yobs and got thumped for his trouble. Julianne thought he deserved it, given how rude he was to her, until she saw him doubled up, an easy target for a bully with nothing better to do than pick on foreigners.

Sometimes, Julianne analysed situations, slices of life, the way she had been taught in her acting classes years ago. She saw that the onlookers thought the redhead was the baddie and were looking forward to the scrap that would make this visit to the Job Centre more interesting than usual. No one was going to intervene. Julianne wondered for a moment whether she should, but knew that would put her in a different kind of spotlight from the one she had wanted to be in. She loved the cinema, but she had always wanted to act in the epic tradition, with the magic of Brecht guiding her step by step. She gave up amateur theatre when her first son was born and had never stepped onto the stage again. It was one of her greatest regrets.

3.

After her hour's wait, Julianne was called into an office with wide windows that admitted no light, only sky threatening rain. She had not brought an umbrella and began to fret because, with her condition, she shouldn't be out in the rain and taxis were beyond her budget. At the other side of the desk, a fat man with a head shaved to hide his bald patch greeted her with a phlegmatic English smile. She took this token attempt at courtesy to mean, Hello, I'm having a bad day, don't get up my nose.

'You have a nice office.'

'Thank you,' he responded, keeping his lips tight.

'I've brought all the paperwork for my pension.'

'Ah – you are Mrs Redgrave, yes?'

'I am. I can't live on what I get, you know?'

'This damn crisis, we're all feeling it.'

'I don't know – those people driving their fancy cars up The Headrow don't seem to be feeling it.'

'Well, they'll be finding things more expensive too.'

'Some people always have ways to get hold of money. I don't. They say 80 percent of us are middle class but there's all kinds of middle class and I'm at the bottom.'

'Look, Mrs Redgrave, you've never paid any contributions. This is the right amount for someone on their own. You have children?'

'They live in London, I can't even afford to get down and see them.'

'That's good, right, I have all your documentation, you should get a decision within a fortnight. Take this. Have a nice day.'

In the waiting room, the Spanish looking youth was about to jump the queue again, but wasn't brave enough to confront the mean looking guy in front of him. Poor lad.

Julianne made her way along Boar Lane as far as McDonalds, where hordes of fourteen-year-olds and half-arsed junior managers devoured their value meals, staring out of the windows, or eating in the street, watching the world go by while cholesterol lined their arteries. The girls wore Nikes and skinny jeans, a postmodern fashion in which things not matching was all that mattered. For some reason, what was just another nouveau style revival, all gaudy mustard and ketchup, set Julianne fuming about how the gears that made the world turn had rusted up.

While Africa needed to mine deadly minerals like coltan to develop, Europe collapsed, and Germany, where a crazy gunman decided to kill everyone he didn't like, lost their edge in precision engineering along with the rest of the industrial world. The economic system, ruled by private capital's endless greed for the dividends that made some individuals richer than many developing countries, was going down the drain. Economia, our modern day God, was sick. The state intervened. Obama and socialists everywhere rubbed their hands in glee.

Briggate was packed. Julianne was allergic to crowds and to fast food joints – the cheap vegetable oil irritated her sinuses. She fled the crush round McDonalds and continued on her way to Kirkgate Market.

4.

Passing through the stench wafting out of KFC set her nose off again. Julianne could not understand how society had become so brainless it could accept shit in breadcrumbs as a meal. Reaching the market she was able to breathe properly again.

Her first stop was always the kiosk by the north door. Julianne loved the tabloids – their exaggeration, sensationalism, the latest topless shenanigans in the Big Brother house, people coming out of the closet. Killing time by living the lives of others, playing the voyeur to blot out your own shortcomings, to give you another set of memories and a different reality to cling on to. Today, The

Sun had breaking news on the country's most important couple, the Beckhams.

Kirkgate Market is massive, over two hundred stalls. Food, drink, music, gifts, car accessories, furniture, ironmongery, pets, joke shops and much more. English working class territory, Turks turning kebabs, Chinese selling office equipment, Pakistani phone stalls, South Africans selling biltong and Caribbeans weaving dreads, all making a huge European Tower of Babel. No parquet and silk ties, no soft suede shoes. Money is humble in Kirkgate Market, because it is shared out between so many, a place even Julianne felt able to spend a little.

The smell of fresh vegetables drew her towards her favourite greengrocer. A lettuce, two pounds of potatoes and a couple of aubergines were what she had in mind, but Steven had a trick of always making you buy more, not that she minded. It made a change to have a friendly conversation with someone with a bit of culture about them. He lived in a village on the outskirts of Leeds with his own allotment and a huge collection of books. The stall was a family business, left to him by his parents. Had he not felt indebted to them and his inheritance he would have been a lawyer, doctor or writer. Meant for greater things, he put up with what he ended up doing by joking, trying to enjoy the work.

'How about three aubergines, Julianne, love?'

'I only need two. But if you tell me what you are reading at the moment I might take another.'

'One of Paul Auster's latest. If you can guess which, I'll give you the third for nowt.'

'Brooklyn Follies.'

'Wow. How did you know?'

'You're like me, you only buy paperbacks and Man in the Dark is only in hardback, so it couldn't be anything else.'

'And you. What are you reading, love?' asked Steven, weighing potatoes.

'Orlando. Virginia Woolf.'

'Mm, Interesting. A little heavy for me.'

'Not for me. I'm with the hermaphrodite, it's all about women, our role.'

'Women aren't human, they're a whole different species. Burroughs.'

'Yes, as soon as our man has gone and we're not bringing up children, not the great earth mother any more, we're nothing. I'm thinking of becoming a lesbian.'

'You should take up your acting again. You could make something of it. I've always seen you as a bit of a Cate Blanchett.'

'If only.'

'Definitely. Look, I have two tickets for a play at the Playhouse tonight. My wife's poorly. If you fancy coming along you'll save me having to flog the ticket.'

'Sir, it would be an honour. What time?'

'Quarter past seven. I'll wait for you by the entrance over there.'

5.

George Street is where the shopping district meets one of the roughest areas of Leeds. At the top end, the shops peter out and shoppers turn back towards the centre. Old pubs like the Three Legs, open from ten in the morning, are taken over by groups of unemployed yobs breakfasting on beer and bacon sandwiches. Stabbings and shootings are common, the hard edge of the city's industrial past. It's full of unemployed junkie families, the sort who drop a sprog every year to receive more state handouts to buy more heroin, foil wraps of ammonium nitrate, their children brought up knowing only violence and deprivation. Problems the government is always trying to solve, always failing. Boredom and truancy create the social sore of marginalisation. Building walkways offer safe areas for dealers selling weed, coke, crack. The mothers stick feeding bottles filled with Pepsi or 7UP in their babies' mouths while the older kids are outside mucking about with their first weapons. George Street marks the boundary between the victims of society and the victims of the economy. Julianne thought that if she were one of this class of parasites, she wouldn't have so many money problems, but she detested drugs, at least the ones you couldn't buy in a chemist.

In this run down part of the city is a warehouse full of cheap clothes fallen out of fashion. Julianne's doctor had recommended her to walk three kilometres a day, and she had been thinking about getting herself a tracksuit.

In 1924, Harold Humphreys brought his tailoring to the sports world by founding Umbro. He has dressed the England team ever since. Umbro is England's brand. There is at least one bit of Umbro kit in most English households. The English like their traditions – they all have fitted carpets, even though there are plenty of more practical floor coverings, and carpets are just filthy dirt magnets. Why change? They say, Can you imagine a real pub without carpets? Julianne thought, it's just like my sons when I ask them why they buy their tracksuits and shirts from Umbro and they say, why give those Yanks at Nike our money, or those Krauts at Adidas?

She saw a sky-blue velour tracksuit she liked so much she left the shop wearing it. The first drops of rain were beginning to fall. Her flat shoes didn't match her new outfit, but were as comfortable as trainers. It was lunchtime. Julianne had planned on going home to eat, but she was too hungry to wait, so instead went into Greggs and bought one of their delicious Cornish pasties, the English empanada. It would keep her going for hours. The English don't sit down for lunch because they don't see eating as a pleasure, more a necessity. If you are hungry, you eat. They have an unwritten rule saying: don't lunch on anything you can't wolf down in thirty seconds. The hours of the day are for working, for productivity, money making, for boosting the economy, making finances flourish so dividends can be pulled like rabbits from a magician's hat.

Julianne had always wanted to go to Cornwall and try an authentic past but, as she couldn't, she forced herself to get used to Greggs' even though she knew they weren't the real thing. Adapt or die. She finished eating, picked up her bags and set off from the storefront she had been sheltering in, towards The Headrow.

6.

Leeds Central Library is a vast Victorian building. Its stone staircase is worth a visit in its own right. Despite her new tracksuit, Julianne's legs were saying enough by the second floor where there were computers for accessing the internet, something she would like to do if only she knew how. She asked for help, but the old hag at the desk told her she needed to book and, anyway, it was not her job to give IT courses. Upset at being talked to so rudely, Julianne snapped Thank you so very much. She wondered if she was being patronised because of her new outfit, so went into the toilet and changed back into her old clothes.

Among the comfy sofas in the ground floor reading

room, she had another go at the computers for searching the library catalogue. She only wanted two books, the digital age could wait. A man about her age was browsing at one of the terminals. He had a grey beard and messy hair. She had a good feeling about him. For some reason the word backwoodsman popped into her head.

'Excuse me, sir, do you know how these work?'

'Well, you could say I am learning.'

'I am only looking for two books, but that grumpy woman at the counter all but called me an idiot for asking her.'

'Don't worry, I can help. What are you looking for?'

'One by Joseph Stiglitz and another by Stanislavski.'

'Do you have a particular title ma'am?' asked the man, politely. He looked Scottish but his accent was pure Yorkshire.

'No, I just want something about economics and I heard him mentioned on the radio, and I want something on acting too.'

'Good. Would you be so kind as to spell the surnames for me please?'

Julianne was so overwhelmed by the man's kindness that it took her a couple of attempts to spell out the names.

'So, economics and theatre, eh? What different worlds.'

'I'm not so sure, Mr…'

'Carragher, but call me Leo.'

'As I was going to say, Mr Leo, maybe they have a lot in common.'

'Yes, yes, certainly. I love the theatre. In fact, I work in the theatre. Would you like to come with me one day?'

Julianne was stunned. Frozen to the spot. She didn't

know how to respond.

'Well, lovely, yes… we must talk about it… I come here a lot… you know?' she managed to stutter nervously. 'I will see you around, I have to go…'

Julianne was shocked – she wasn't used to this. Her chatty nature and love of talking to strangers seemed to have backfired on her, but what could she do? Alone in the world, her only pleasure came from talking to friendly people she met out and about. This man had appeared charming, fine. Maybe his intentions hadn't been bad, perhaps the invitation had not been serious, maybe he was just being polite, but the situation had slipped out of control. She needed time to think about it.

As she fled she heard the man call after her, 'I am sorry, madam. I did not mean to be so blunt.'

7.

All aflutter with nerves and adrenalin from the library incident, she decided to walk home despite her shopping bags. She felt nothing. Not the rain, not her aching legs. As she walked she began to feel guilty. She played and replayed what had happened. The rain intensified but she plodded on, confused by how such an agreeable situation had turned on its head. He liked you, idiot, he liked you, she said over and over. Her complexes, her fears left her helpless, like a fifteen-year-old meeting her first boyfriend, totally lost, unable to be herself. She needed to act, she had to act. She remembered her theatre classes; when you play a role, you have to fill the space of somebody unknown.

The actor needs to know everything about the character, their conflicts, their situation, their worries – you have to fill the blank sheet of their psychological makeup, ask questions constantly. But Julianne didn't have anybody to ask her questions of.

Once home, she made up her mind to go back to the library as soon as she had decided what to wear to the theatre. She was soaked, and had started to sneeze. The day would be a complete failure if she didn't make the play. Her clothes for special occasions lay moth-eaten deep in her wardrobe, like the dress she wore at a service to commemorate those who fell in the Falklands, a bright marine blue number by Hobbs she bought second-hand in York. She hadn't tried it on for years, the zip probably wouldn't even do up and she had no one to help her. To ask John, her drama queen of a neighbour, would just create another situation like the one in the library.

She was alone. Totally alone. The old dears in her circle were withering in the face of spring. They were candles in a lighting shop, typewriters in Silicon Valley, scythes in a John Deere showroom. Useless, obsolete, out of date. And me? wondered Julianne, I'm the same, but friendlier.

Abandoning her idea of returning to the library, she had two and a half hours to kill before the theatre and decided to eat her dinner in front of the TV.

8.

She didn't eat much, though – her nerves had dented her appetite. She was still unsettled by the incident in the library. Not so much by what had happened, but because she had opened up her Pandora's Box of sadness, fears, ghosts and frustrations. She didn't know if she would ever see this Mr Carragher again, but if she did she would be sure to show herself as a women who was completely different to the idiot that had acted so ridiculously in the library. She had nothing to lose.

The sun was setting, evening fell across the city. Typical, just when there was hardly any daylight left, the sun came out. Unbelievable. Days when it was supposed to be warm were even worse, like the sun was so embarrassed to be out, it rushed its appearance into as short a time as possible. The English don't go in for outdoor swimming pools, it is easier to get to the sea. The coast is not far from Leeds. One of the widows from her coffee morning had a house near Hull. They'd all been invited several times, but none of them would budge from home. Julianne would have liked to have gone, most of all because it was roughly in the direction of Scarborough. She remembered its fishing boats, a casino on the beach. A summer holiday place she had always thought of as her Cape Cod like in Norman Mailer's novel Tough Guys Don't Dance. Scarborough was where she and her husband first had sex. The first time they had left Leeds together, on their honeymoon trip through England and Scotland. The best of her life. Since then, her confidence had drained away as their lovemaking became little more than her husband pumping away on her, better when he was drunk but still sex without feeling, without desire, without hitting the spot.

It was nearly six by the time she had showered and had begun to sort her hair out. Her courage was beginning to return. She had looked in the mirror several times and was even ready to put on a little lipstick. She didn't even know what play they were going to see, but the greengrocer's invitation had given her a boost. Steven thought of her as an interesting woman worth talking to. He was much younger and obviously not attracted to her, but intellectually they had something they both held dear. It could be the start of something special.

LS3

1.

The same question bugs me every afternoon, You work, then what? Yesterday was no exception. Every day I panic. DVDs, football and PlayStation are all I have outside work. I don't even go to the Hispanic community socials.

When the alarm buzzes I leap out of bed feeling happy. I am going spend eight hours with my little chicks. I'd rather spend eight hours with them than with most of the people on this planet. I make myself a proper English breakfast, then I am ready… for work.

If you grow up on the border between Colombia and Ecuador you're going to be a determined kind of guy. My mother died in childbirth. I was brought up – little

Andres – by my Dad, a FARC commander. I am a child of FARC, of the Armed Forces of the Colombian Revolution, the product of a night of partying and the rape of hostages. Many children have been conceived in the Colombian jungle. Fruits of desire on some occasions, sometimes the fruit of accidents. The children of FARC, brought up between hand grenades and Kalashnikovs. An old, unloaded semi-automatic was my first toy.

Leaving this inbred, loveless paternal tyranny from another age was not easy. When I was twelve I escaped the camp and crossed into Ecuador. Once I reached Quito, my real adventure began. I had to build my life from scratch – a rebirth – until I reached a point where my past beyond the Orinoco no longer seemed to exist. And now, at almost forty, having achieved social and economic stability, here I am asking myself what else is there? You work, then what?

I have always adapted to the people I am among. I have developed an instinct for survival and a silver tongue that gets me anything I want. Almost anything. But there was something else that became more and more difficult. The jungle killed my libido. A whack in the balls, or some reptile bite, some guerrilla drugs, I have no idea. During puberty maybe I had some kind of condition that disconnected my sexual drive. I didn't feel the need to lose my virginity, nothing about sex attracted me in any way and before I ended up on this island I never had sex with anybody. It was only then that I asked myself, Where is my partner, my better half, the person who I can share my problems with? Maybe I had put too much into survival and lost other skills, like loving.

My libido eventually turned up soon after I arrived in England. In general, the English, especially if they are drunk, treat relationships so frivolously that anybody would have been able to lose the fear I had. Lilly, a hot blond doctor, daughter of some rich businessman, stripped me of my virginity. She fucked me out on the stairs. I say she fucked me because I was a puppet in her hands, or between her legs more like. When it finished, about three minutes after it started, she said, I barely noticed that, come in, relax and warm yourself up for another. And it was like that all night – her favourite pastime, shagging. By dawn I had finally begun to grasp some kind of sexual technique. I could have gone on all day. But Lilly, once satisfied, put her thong back on and was gone with the morning. Since then I have been different. I can only think of Lilly and the love she could give me. I wish I could convert my memories of her into something more solid than wanting something that has already happened.

Everyone has a film that tells the story of their life. In mine, the Colombian government and the paramilitaries were the baddies that had to be stood up to, kidnapped, tortured, killed without pity. I didn't like the plot, so I changed it for another, based on me looking for my place in the world. I dragged myself through the streets of Quito, lived on a permanent high in Guayaquil, took a boat to Panama City and, finally, decided to settle in San Jose, Costa Rica. There I had a lot of time to think and decided on Mexico as the next stop on the path north to the USA. I worked in Tegucigalpa until I had saved enough cash to cross the border. Days later I woke up in Puebla, another step towards the new world.

2.

I struggle to make sense of my life, my forty years of travelling beyond the blood, sweat and smell of shrapnel. We live in a paradox, battling to get work we don't even want. You need to work to get cash, status, a place on the capitalist ladder, even if it's just the bottom rung, but society does not distribute jobs according to people's capacity to do them. If it was like that, you'd not have so many people who hate work.

In the jungle I learnt a lot about animals, and I learned more inseminating horses on a stud in New Mexico. Then I studied Veterinary Science for two years in Madrid and finished my degree here in England. Straight after graduating I got a job at Tropical World, a little animal park on the edge of Leeds. But my nice little job didn't last long. The boss was Lilly's dad, a heavyweight member of the BNP. He caught us by the park exit, with our tongues down each other's throats, and fired me on the spot. My only relationship ruined my life, so how could I see having one as anything positive? Lilly still calls every now and then, asking me over. She is a witch. But for some reason, I always agree to see her.

Today is the 21st March, another day of my life, one day less until my death. It is half eight in the morning and I am heading to Morley in the suburbs of the city and the chicken farm where I work sexing chicks. I distinguish between male and female birds so that they can be separated according to their use: as breeders, for meat, for laying, etc. The skill of the sexer is to be able to quickly tell the difference in gender by touch – something imperceptible to anyone else.

I live in the centre of Leeds, in what they call town. Right near the train station. Every day I catch a local train to Morley. In England, the metropolitan areas are divided up into districts. Some of these areas are almost like small towns in their own right. The districts in Leeds each have their own codes. I live in LS1, Morley is LS27. Although part of the city, it is also a market town from way back in medieval times when some places were granted the right to hold markets. Morley was once popular with young people – one of the birthplaces of European clubbing culture. Until it closed, The Orbit electronica club was a mecca for clubbers from all over.

Not so long ago I met a Catalan guy who also works in

Morley – Richard. He's a bit of a weirdo. He refuses to hang out with other Spaniards, says they're all a ball ache. He thinks Catalans are too, though less so. According to Richard, the Spanish are just a bunch of nouveau rich plebs who still piss in their gardens. What's more, he says the Spanish middle class stink of rancid nationalism, while he loves talking politics and trashing whatever society he finds himself in. It's been two days now that I have been avoiding him. We had a little chat about FARC and I lost my temper. I'd really prefer not to see him.

Today, the train is quieter than usual. It is not going to be easy to avoid the Catalan. I use the old trick of hiding behind a tabloid. The train sets off.

'Hey! Dude! I didn't see you there. Are you hiding from me or what?'

Shit, I thought I was going to avoid this little turd today. I am seriously thinking of changing to the nightshift. This loser is really starting to piss me off and I'm beginning to think he fancies me. Today he's putting it out more than ever.

'You've cut your hair! You look good. Eh, handsome?'

I glance at him. He sits down and thumps me on the arm so I have to lower my paper.

I snarl, 'I'm reading how the paramilitaries have attacked a FARC camp.'

'Cool, but we're not going to be like the other day are we, Andy? Everybody is entitled to their own views, you know? And for me, FARC are a bunch of shitty terrorists, always have been.'

'I never said they weren't terrorists. Killers, sure. But have you never wondered why they exist? Don't you see how some elected presidents in South American are just military dictators in disguise? Don't you think we have to fight that?'

'Ha – don't talk to me about resistance! If you came from Catalonia you'd know all about Spanish imperialism.'

'It's always the same with you. You know nothing. You fancy a holiday in Juarez City, eh? You can have anything you want there, and more. Don't fuck with me. Have the military taken over Catalonia, by any chance? Have you heard about Señor Matanza, Mr Massacre, eh?'

'Sure man, yeh Andres, don't get worked up.'

'Have you heard of Señor Matanza or not?'

'Sure man, from the song by Manu Chao.'

'By Mano Negra Do you know who Señor Matanza is?'

'Then no, not really, someone to do with FARC...'

'Not exactly. Listen to the song. Then you'll maybe you'll understand what I am saying...'

I raise the newspaper to carry on reading like I was before this fuckwit turned up, but can't concentrate with him constantly buzzing in my ears. He's annoyed, glances about without fixing on anything. I sneak a look. I thought he was an airhead, socially inept, and sooner or later I would just have to tell him to fuck off, seeing as he couldn't take a hint. But I was wrong. This time I had hurt his feelings. I think he actually likes me. I turn to the sports pages – Liverpool are facing Chelsea in the quarter finals of the Champions League.

3.

The train speeds up, Richard still doesn't say anything. I'm tempted just to ask him to find another seat but guess from his silence that he has finally got the situation. But I'm wrong.

'Hey Andy, changing the subject, how's it going sexing these chicks? I've heard you stick your little finger up their arses?'

I have to admit that what he says and the way he says it makes me laugh sometimes. The floor is slippery with the bullshit that pours from his mouth.

'Ha, that's funny. Fuck, we are famous all over, us chicken sexers.'

'So do you have to or not?'

'Fine, OK, there are various ways to sex them, by the wing, by the arse or by colour. But mostly the arse.'

'But come on, tell me, what can you feel up the bum of a chick?'

'What?'

'What's different in a male to a female?'

'Ah, that. Well, it's a different musculature, you can't see their bits.'

'Wow, you're amazing. How long does it take?'

'Four seconds.'

'Wow, so in an hour, your rate must be phenomenal, no?'

'More than a thousand birds an hour, but the Japanese, they can do a lot more.'

'Fuck me. You like your work? There can't be many sexers in the world, eh?'

'Depends. In Japan there's loads.'

'You'll go on to be a Master Sexer, eh!'

'Go on, laugh. Sexers are in demand and the pay's good. For me it is OK, but I am a vet, I'd much rather be doing that.'

'Yeh, and I'm a solicitor and hate my work, but at least I am in an office and don't have to smell shit…'

'You take the job that gives you the cash to live. I've found the one that pays the most. I bet I enjoy mine more than you.'

The train slows and finally the guard announces we are arriving in Morley. Richard heads for his office and me to my chickens. He leaves looking miserable, I leave whistling. The sky threatens rain.

A couple of weeks ago they took on a new sexer. A Peruvian with a Japanese mother and a rate of 1200 chicks an hour. He can't be more than twenty-five but he already thinks he's the big chief. He is an arrogant cock-sucking prick with whom I have had a few run-ins and when I enter the changing room he's flexing his biceps and admiring his six-pack in the mirror.

'Hey, mate, yesterday I nailed 1500. Beat that,' he says.

'That's nothing, I've done that thousands of times.'

'Not that I've seen.'

'OK, you're the best, you get the medal.'

'Can't take the competition, eh? You're scared.'

'Yeh, your Nip face scares me.'

'And you're a fucking racist.'

'So what, you going to smack me?'

'You're a loser. You've been here a year already and daren't compete with me.'

I hate competitiveness in the workplace. We have to work hard to get cash. But to compete against fellow employees just to climb the company ladder is something that, when you've risked your life just to get hold of any old shitty job, I simply cannot comprehend. I'm sick of workers who sell themselves to their bosses, who put out their foot to trip up their colleagues when the boss is around, who think there isn't room for two top dogs. I work, do the best job I can, then go home. That's it. But this fucking prick is winding me up so much that I am going to have to rise to him. I don't have his dexterity, his Japanese speed, but I am sure that my error rate is much less than his.

'Fine, little Jappo, I accept.'

'OK. We're going for the highest number.'

'Against the number of errors. Errors are subtracted from the final total, OK?'

4.

No need for a whistle, we kick off right away. The Peruvian plays like an Argentinian; dirty, to win at any price. He sexes chickens without shutting his trap, his greasy Latino voice rabbiting on through his mask. He just won't shut up, like he's picking at a sore, irritating me.

'I love the tight little cunts in your country, Andy, but you don't look like you enjoy eating them, right?'

'It doesn't say in the rules I have to talk to you, you little shit, so shut your dirty Jap mouth.'

'The ones from Pereira are the best. You know what makes them so hot?'

'They're like God meant them to be, with round eyes,

not squinty eyed cunts like you.'

'You've gone too far, you piece of shit.'

I stop, leave off sexing chicks and square up to him.

'Insult me again and I'll smash your face in.'

'Suck my dick, I'm over 200…'

Killing somebody means nothing to me. I killed two paramilitaries and a civilian with a hand grenade. No one told me to do it. I came across them one night, spying on the FARC camp. Everyone was asleep, but I was up with a dodgy stomach. If they had seen me they would have shot me. I was twelve. I took the grenade, pulled the pin and threw it as hard as I could into the undergrowth where they were hiding. Three dead. I strangled a man in Guatemala and killed another with a blade in Sonora. I'm trained in boxing and martial arts, but for years now I have avoided trouble. It's been ages since I've had to use my fighting skills – I was happy to give them up as soon as I arrived in the UK.

For a time in Madrid, I had no choice but to do a stint as a gangster because I needed to pay for my studies and get my papers sorted. I knew a group of Colombians who worked as mules for the Medellin cartel in Spain. At the end of the nineties they made good money selling adulterated coke into the Madrid party crowd and every now and then a job came up that was a bit more complicated. They were professionals, I didn't fear the police. I accepted work in 'the kitchen', cutting the coke in the secret labs on the outskirts of Madrid. I matriculated at University while working discreetly for the clan. In exchange they supplied me with the British passport which made me a European citizen.

A little while later, the boss chose me for a job that was more serious, working with another outfit. They were an all-Spanish gang known as The Miami. Nowadays their name only lives on in legend, but in the nineties you only had to mention The Miami in Madrid and people would shit themselves. The Miami quickly developed their black market operation and established a network that involved everyone, even the police and lawyers. Their closeness to the Colombian cartels gave their leaders a status in Spain that no organised crime outfit has had since, a whole universe of power in the hands of a few leaders, still so young.

In 2000 they bought me a ticket for the Santander to Southampton ferry. I have never returned to Spain. Each time I feel the killer instinct stir in me again, I remember how The Miami ended up, drowned in their own bile.

5.

After the invitation to suck his cock and a long silence, things seem to calm down. I don't say a word. I'm thinking of The Miami. I pretend that things have cooled down, it's much better like this. Here at work they don't know who I am. Although I try hard to deny it, deep down I'm a killer, an assassin. It is my nature.

'400 hundred, twat, I've done 400. And you?'

'Fewer, but that means fewer mistakes. I am not worried by you, dickhead.'

'I told you, don't insult me.'

He straightens up, looking serious, and pulls up his right sleeve, flexes his biceps and says, like Clint Eastwood in

Heartbreak Ridge, 'You want to see who can fist the most in a minute?'

I look at him. He's a joke, almost too stupid to be real. But he is real – the shit he talks proves it. Men, unlike women, reach a point where they are so wound up they can't move on without violence. When the words get to them one bloke or the other will kick off in order to finish the fight as quickly and cleanly as possible. The Peruvian and I have arrived at this point. He clouds my vision, my brain lacks oxygen and my predator's instinct surges like volcanic pressure. It's like an eruption, an opening of my insides to release the instincts that have lain dormant from another time in my life. Without responding to his slit-ty-eyed offer, I stand up, turn my back on him and taking a plank that's leaning against the wall, spin and hit him over and over in the face. Once he's on the floor I really go at him, angry, sadistic, until I realise that his face is just a red mess and it's impossible to make out his features. I notice he's still breathing but any more whacks above his shoulders would finish him off, so I concentrate on his ribs. The crack of each bone fracturing sounds beautiful. I follow up on his legs and spine. There is nowhere left to hit him, he is like a junkie with no veins left to shoot up into, just a breathing corpse. Someone grabs me from behind, various people hurl themselves on me. They restrain me, I don't fight back. The supervisor and other workers shout at me, You've killed him, you've killed him. Not true, the fucking little shit is still alive. Things calm down and they call an ambulance. They've got me pinned down. I say I need to go to the toilet to throw up and the supervisor escorts me like a prisoner to the electric chair. As soon as

I've closed the door and slid the bolt shut I am out of the window. I don't stop running until I'm at the train station. It's raining.

So what. I'll look for another job. There are plenty of chicken farms round Leeds. I made a mistake that I will have to accept, though I'm pissed off how I let the situation get out of hand. I fell into the trap of a cocky little cunt looking for a war. I have already been in too many situations like this, but instincts are something you carry inside and are impossible to change. My reality, the places I've been, my memories... I can't think of my life without them, almost as if killing is in my genes. My father killed men, hung them, burnt them. Without pity. No remorse. They say we all have to live with the guilt that comes with original sin that codes and religions impose on us. I don't ask moral questions. I act before I think. I survive. Because of this, I don't need to purge my sins to feel OK about myself. I only need to begin anew, change into civilised guy, a citizen who lives in peace without messing with anybody, and with no one messing with him. I'm a rational animal just looking to survive, same as a cat or an ape. I am a man, a cold killer, a demi-god with the right to decide on the life of those around me. Us human beings are a unique species. We have the capacity to self-destruct. We are dangerous. Unnatural.

6.

It's four in the afternoon. I pay six quid for a greasy Burger King and five minutes later I'm through the Dark Arches and in my flat. I open the logo covered bag and see they've cheated me. No chips. Michael Douglas in Falling Down pops into my head, but my problems are off his scale; I'm still resigning myself to my half-a-meal deal when The Verve's Bitter Sweet Symphony makes me jump. My ringtone. My boss is trying to get hold of me. I need an hour's headspace, it's best not to deal with these things until they have cooled down. I decide not to answer. I hope he won't call the police. With all the migrants he employs, it wouldn't be in his interests if he did.

I finish eating, click on the box and drift off in front of a BBC documentary. The hypnotic voiceover goes in one ear and out of the other. I float into limbo. All the arguing, the fighting exhausts you, sucks out all your energy, pulls you under.

I'm woken by another burst of The Verve. I screw up my eyes at the screen. My boss again. He doesn't have the balls to ring the police. Fuck off. Sleeping has given me a headache. My eyes are pounding. Ibuprofen is the answer. In my medicine bag I find a plastic bag full of something like black dung. It is a mushroom. I remember – a magic mushroom Lilly gave me. She's obsessed with mind control. She's strange, frightening at times. She goes on about how if you take Yage you can read the minds of the people around you. She's a manipulating liar. She controls my free will with her tits and pussy. She knows exactly how to play me. She knows how that night she marked me for life. I daren't eat the magic mushroom whole, so I go to tear a piece off but end up with half of it, and chew. I have no idea what kind the mushroom is or how powerful, whether it'll make me feel good or crazy. I swallow.

Burroughs. Lilly's always going on about a writer called Burroughs, tells me how he was obsessed with ayahuasca and mind control. According to Lilly, everybody's being controlled by those who hold the strings: political parties, advertising, propaganda, religion, money. All crap. Advertising exists to make you believe that some piece of consumer shit you never had any use for is suddenly indispensable in your life. It's false, all lies, a trick that we all end up believing. Money is still our god, the mechanism that drives almost everything, the thing that motivates everyone. It's abstract, without value. Monopoly money, the lot of it. We kill each other for nothing more than paper. The financial system is virtual, like the internet, like social media, chat rooms. We live in an apparently comfortable world of 'wellbeing' whose objective is happiness – but it is an imposed happiness; our gurus peddle a false joy that sweeps everything under the carpet. Faith has manipulated the human mind for centuries, but it has had a field day since liberalism took the reins.

Lilly taught me all this. According to her, Burroughs, a junkie dropout, reached God, the Truth, the Universe though drugs. His writings uncover the lies by which we live, how we've castrated of our animal instincts – the only part of us that is capable of rebelling.

I fall back on the sofa, find Radio Caracol on satellite. The screen is black. I listen to a Shakira song saying something about a blind, deaf and dumb brute and see something in the LCD, a clear image emerging between the layers of the screen. It looks like Uncle Sam. He wears a stars and stripes top hat and a waistcoat. He has a white chinstrap beard, no moustache. A Yankee. He emerges as far as the second screen layer, fixes me with his eyes, points with the forefinger of his left hand and says, You. He raises his right hand towards his chin and spits out pieces of broken teeth. From a little pile of tusks, he picks a gold molar, shows it me and smiles. Then is gone.

My mind moves with the speed of light. My thoughts are not thoughts, only reflections of what I am thinking, like a photo stream. I hear techno music, a mix I like. My thoughts strobe, and I remember yesterday I dreamt I broke all my teeth. My flashing thoughts become a chain of images flying past, the other half of my brain mixes doses of fantasy and reality. I see Lilly. She is working in the old people's home. She does not have much to do. She never has much to do. She's looking through a microscope, examining something. Some drug, surely, some type of hallucinogenic. I feel a negative atmosphere in the home. Something strange is happening there. I have lost all sense of time in my hallucinatory state. I have no idea what shit is going to happen in the old people's place, but I know for the first time I want something more from her – concern, a cherishing, I want to protect her. Something is changing. I look at my watch, it's nearly six in the evening. I pick up my keys and some cash and go out. The home is in LS6, near Headingley Stadium. I flag down a cab.

7.

I agree the fare with the Pakistani driver. They love to pimp their cars – this is one powered with rocket fuel, souped up with a Moma rally steering wheel and gear stick. The red Recaro front seats are branded Citroen. I ask about them.

'With these seats, brother, these actual seats, Sebastian Loeb won his first World Rally Championship.'

If he wasn't a Pakistani I would have thought he was joking, but as I said, they love their cars, their tuning, their pimping up. It's possible that these seats carry Loeb's DNA, but the speed with which we take Woodhouse Lane makes me think it's not only Loeb's DNA in the car but his spirit too. I should ask him to slow down, but secretly

I'm enjoying the speed.

In Headingley Lane there are radars, he slows down. The cars are at a standstill. Not for the speed cameras, but some other hold up. Nothing moves, we're just sat there. I'm getting nervy, tell him I'm in a hurry. He says that there's nothing he can do about it. I tell him to turn round, but he points to the solid line of traffic. We hear an ambulance coming from behind us. Cars part to let it through.

'Here's good!' I tell him. 'Take half, let me out here.'

'No, you can't,' he says nervously, 'we've agreed the price. It'll cost you the same whatever, you can't pay me half.'

'Course I can, we didn't sign anything. I am giving you more than it would cost to here, so don't give me any ball ache.'

I throw three quid onto the passenger seat and get out, whistling. It'll only take me ten minutes to walk. I am beginning to come down from my high, so I can just about walk the street without anyone knowing I am not on the same planet.

I come across the accident a little further down. One of the cars is burning. I walk right by so I don't have to cross the road and a policeman shouts at me, Are you crazy? Get the fuck out of there. I am still off my head so it doesn't occur to me that the car might explode. I give him the finger. In Colombia this could cost you your life but he doesn't pay any attention. I carry on walking to Otley Road, where the Headingley shops are. Nothing in my head but seeing Lilly. I have no idea how she will react to me turning up but I need to see her, need to find out whether this feeling is love. Since I was provoked into attacking the Peruvian I have believed in love. For the first time. Being human must be like this – when you feel alone, when everything is shit, you put your ego to one side and seek company, protection, affection. Support. I am feeling this. Maybe it is an illusion or because I'm high. I don't know. All I know is I want sex again.

I go up Otley Road to Wood Lane. The sirens are still wailing. A bittersweet symphony, like the song, like my ringtone, like my phone conversations, like my life. A little along Wood Lane there's another accident. Two police cars and two ambulances block the street. The crash must have been spectacular, much more impact than the other though there's no fire. A jazzed up red Ford Focus has inserted itself into a yellow Beatle. Someone is zipping up one of those black body bags that mean only one thing. The street isn't very wide, there's a bend, the Focus must have been going at some speed to make such an impact. The sight is amazing, so I stop a while listening to what people are saying. A young couple are explaining to the police how the two guys in the red car had fled the scene even though they'd been injured. The police tell them they know the car belongs to a known offender. They ask about the other one, the passenger. The women seems really anxious and the man says that he was distracted while calling the emergency services and didn't see him run off, but he looked foreign, maybe Italian or Spanish. Thirty-ish, tall, thin, tanned, with gelled back hair.

The home is not far from the accident, hidden behind trees. Lilly probably knows nothing about any of this. It's not quite night yet and the light's fading.

8.

A little further up the street I reach the entrance to the home. The body bag has made me think. I feel tiny, like an ant in a football stadium. Dwarfed. I have killed a lot of people but no one has killed me. I can't put myself in the place of my victims, I can't empathise with them, can't feel anything for that shit-head Peruvian. But I realise from the effects of the mushroom how fleeting life is, how you can lose your life in a tenth of a second, without knowing it, unexpected, a surprise. It happens all the time, no chance to prepare, or get used to the idea. Bang. A moment and you are gone.

So then what's the fucking point of it? What will I

leave on this earth? What will have been the point of my existence? All these doubts fly around my head. I feel my high trickling away through my fingertips. I am tired and confused. I hope Lilly can answer some of these questions, I hope she'll give me a blow job.

Night falls over Leeds. It hasn't started raining again but the atmosphere is grey, sad, hopeless. One of the street-lamps is broken and the sickly orange light of the other two is not enough to light up the entrance to the home. I fumble around the gate, bend down to find the handle and get smacked on the nose. I don't fall and straighten up, shocked. Someone leaving has banged into me.

'Oh, sorry.'

A young guy, in his thirties. His nose is bandaged up so I can hardly see his face. Olive skinned, curly hair. He looks Mediterranean.

'Español, amigo?'

'I'm in a rush,' he answers in Spanish, 'I'm in a hurry. I am sorry if I hurt you, mate.'

The guy slips past me and jogs off in the opposite direction to the crash. I wonder if he was the guy who abandoned the red Focus. I bend down again to find the handle in the gloom, and see a bit of paper on the ground. I pick it up. A theatre ticket, March 21st at 7.45, the West Yorkshire Playhouse. I like the name of the play and think that if Lilly doesn't come up with a better offer, I'll go along. I have never been to the theatre. I'm nervous, jumpy, all het up. In this state I enter the home.

'Hello love, how's it going?'

'Bad, Lilly, very bad. I fought a guy at work, nearly killed him. I ate that mushroom that you gave me, been tripping for a while. There's things I saw coming here, I've no idea if they were real. Two bad accidents within a kilometre.'

'Don't worry, honey, it was only a little mushroom. I doubt it would have you seeing things. You can't be here now, you know my Dad drops by.'

'Yeh, I know, Lilly, only I had this dream. You were in danger, a man covered in blood came here, threatened you.'

'You're not that far off, he just left. The only thing that is threatening now is you, you're all over the place.'

'I'm sorry, I'm worrying too much. I've had a shit day. You know? You're the only person I could come to.'

Lilly comes over and kisses my cheek, then on my neck and finally my lips. I have a hard-on and suggest she locks the surgery door for a fuck.

'You're crazy! My Dad's about to arrive.'

'Fine, Lilly, then I'm going to the theatre.'

'The theatre! You never go to the theatre. What's on?'

'I don't remember.'

'Romeo and Juliet maybe! I don't know why you're being such a softy today, usually you're such a tough guy.'

'Maybe hard types don't dance, but they can still fall in love.'

'Come on honey, you're just emotional.'

'No Lilly, listen. Life's a bitch, it's shit, especially mine. Battle after battle just to get enough cash to live. And once you get it, all you have is emptiness, a black hole, tedium, monotony. What's left except staring at SKY all day, death's waiting room? I'm sorry Lilly, but you, yes you – recently you've been the only thing that has given me any happiness. There's nothing, no one I love more than you. But seeing how you treat me, memories are all I've got now.'

'It's OK Andres, it's fine. Calm down. Of course I feel something for you. I don't know quite what, but there's something that brings us together. We should just...'

Her father's voice booms along the corridor. He's talking with the nurse, trying to flirt with bad jokes and cheesy pick-up lines.

'The backdoor, Andres. Look, I'll call you tomorrow and we can have a drink and talk and who knows... My old man is here. Go.'

'I love you Lilly.'

LS6

1.

Are you ready to tell us everything, Mr Carragher? asked the older of the two policemen.

It was not that simple. Although a veteran in the battle of life, Leo had never seen anything like this. In a fraction of a second the West Yorkshire Playhouse had been blown apart. So much blood, death and destruction, but, incredibly, he was still alive. An emergency nurse asked Leo to take off his shirt so he could assess the extent of his injuries. Leo felt nothing, just shock. An unbearable ringing in his ears, two strands of blood hanging from his nostrils. The policemen asked the nurse to be as quick as possible. Leo did not know where to look, nor what to say, or what to make of this moment.

In an explosion, energy is transformed at great velocity. There is a phase of supersonic combustion. To the human brain, time stands still. A window opens into a new dimension in which, in the tiniest fraction of time, natural material is transformed into molecules. Leo was lucky – even though he was not able to process what had happened, his molecular structure remained intact. Moments from his student days flew through his mind. His childhood, his adolescence, becoming a young man. His life passed in sequence: being born in Pisa, studying physics at Bologna University, his mother's death, abandoning his studies and moving to Leeds with his father. That was the last thing he remembered.

By some miracle, a poster of Salvador Dali's Atomic Leda, which had been hung across the foyer together with other iconic paintings, was still intact. Atomic Leda depicted a naked female figure modelled on Gala, the painter's wife, suspended in the air with a swan. The composition was based on the golden bough, its figures placed geometrically in the mystical Pythagorean pentagram by an artist searching for a perfect harmony based on natural law. The Greeks and the Renaissance painters had an ideal of beauty in which all dimensions were in proportion to each other. All art – architecture in particular – had always been influenced by the golden number known as Phi, a Greek letter representing the natural process of the Universe, the internal mechanism by which it maintained its stability and balance.

When Leo arrived in Leeds, the balance in England was changing. In the early seventies immigration was rising and the first tensions began to appear with the growing Pakistani population. Leo had to give up his Physics studies because his father's retirement meant he had to work. He found a job in a cinema; first he tore tickets on the door, then became an usher and after fifteen years of saving he bought the crumbling hundred and fifty seat Casablanca. But with the arrival of Thatcherite liberalism came the big multinationals who destroyed all his years of hard work. The Casablanca Cinema finally closed its doors in 1988 and Leo found himself working as an usher again, but this time for a big American chain. Despite all his experience he had to sit through a humiliating interview in which a girl barely into her twenties decided whether he was up to the job. Leo did not adapt well to the changes his new country underwent in the eighties. People like him who had worked for twenty years were treated by the nouveau riche as little more than labourers.

From the sale of The Casablanca and his wage as an usher Leo put enough aside to get married. He and his wife had a son, but both mother and child died during the birth. Leo didn't fall into depression, neither did his character change. His study of physics led him to an understanding of the natural world and a belief that where science ended, faith began, and that faith was what you held on to when you couldn't find the answers to your questions. Leo was certain that everything was explained somewhere in books, that we have a destiny and that there was some purpose in the death of his wife and son. He believed in the golden bough, in proportion and balance. He felt life owed him something. His only fear was that he would die before he found out what that was.

2.

At nine o'clock on the evening of the 21st March 2009, the West Yorkshire Playhouse was shaken by a huge explosion. News crews rushed to the scene. The whole nation was glued to the television. Total confusion. The first theory, a terrorist attack, faded by the minute as the first survivors who had been sitting in the highest seats gave their accounts. The facts began to point to a gas explosion. Twenty-three dead already, but the number rose by the minute.

Smoke billowed from the main doors. On a huge charred billboard The Death of Margaret Thatcher could still be made out. The piece, by English playwright Tom Green, examined how the death of the ex-Prime Minister would affect different characters, like a northern miner who had walked south just to spit on her grave. The play caused controversy up and down the country.

The theatre, behind the bus station near the train line, was a modern, safe building so no one suspected a gas leak until some broken pipes were discovered behind an internal wall. The lower part of the stalls had been completely obliterated and several members of the cast killed. They died while representing death. Fiction became reality.

As Leo regained consciousness, he absorbed the facts. He was sitting on the foyer floor, an oxygen mask over his face. A chill ran through his body and he slipped into a blissful tranquillity, a state of absolute resignation. He felt he could expect nothing more than this – he had taken everything life had thrown at him, and now, in his old age, he just wanted peace and, you never know, there might even something better to come.

As a youngster in Italy, Leo was brought up with strong Christian beliefs, but just before he moved to Bologna to study, he became convinced that science superseded faith. He wanted to know how much of this great grey area had a human explanation before throwing himself in. He wanted to learn, so enrolled in the Faculty of Physics where he specialised in quantum mechanics. Leo understood the Universe to be a space which regulated its own forces. He was an empiricist, believing everything had a reason. But despite all the equations he was left sensing the existence of a supreme being who tests our faith. Leo spent his years of Catholicism searching for Platonic ideals, staring into a sky where the angels had already lost themselves in the great blue emptiness. All his theories turned on the same axis. Heraclitus. Aristotle. St Thomas of Aquinas. Hume. Nietzsche. Everything is the same, all is circular, everything repeats itself indefinitely in a spatial-temporal sequence that the human mind can't grasp.

Twenty one grams lighter, Leo was helped to his feet, thinking for some reason of an uncle in Tokyo. Another emigrant. Once he was on his feet he looked around, and with the 10 percent of his brain still functioning, asked himself, why am I still here?

3.

Having esoteric knowledge of quantum mechanics and earning your living by showing people to their cinema seats can end up being pretty frustrating. But Leo had been made to get used to this right from the start, when as a young man deciding what he was going to do with his life he told his father that he wanted to study physics. His father, an old man made sullen and bitter by his self-inflicted loneliness, spat out one of the phrases that made Leo hate him, Never dedicate yourself to the thing you love most, you will stop enjoying it. So Leo accepted his passion for physics was to be a hobby, never his profession. His father died a few years later but Leo never did manage to free himself from the heavy yoke of mindless work.

Books were his refuge. His parallel universe. His strength. He swapped philosophical essays for the stories of Borges and replaced Rousseau and Marx with Huxley and Orwell. He never put them down. For him, fiction explained reality and through books he began to understand the truths of the world he slowly withdrew from, buying a little house just outside Morley a few kilometres from the city. Some of his neighbours thought he was crazy, just a hippie trying to be self-sufficient, trying to get by without entering the rat race. He had the craggy looks from his father's side of the family, who had originally come from Scotland, and gradually the years whitened his hair and beard, wrinkled his features even more. Leo had a year of working left and was looking forward to having proper time to think, a new life, retirement. He planned to buy some chickens, grow vegetables. He was joining local clubs and societies to do with his interests and didn't entirely discount the possibility that he might even find somebody to share the rest of his life with.

Film remained another of his passions. But in his free time he didn't want anything that reminded him of his work – his way of keeping his head above water. So Leo never went to the movies. He liked to remember his childhood in Pisa, ducking down in the first row of the Cinema Milano for a crafty fag. Italian neo-realism and the classics. He could run whole films in his memory, recite stretches of dialogue parrot fashion. From time to time he watched films on his 32 inch plasma TV, but what he really liked were the made-for-TV series. He considered them the cinema of the future. Films which lasted hours and hours, whole sagas in the three seasons of a series. He loved Prison Break, House and Lost.

He woke to a buzzing in his ears and a throbbing headache. Leo sat up, feeling dizzy and realised that last night he had fallen asleep in his living room. He knew he shouldn't have tried to watch five episodes in one sitting. It was 8 AM on the 21st March 2009.

Morley is a quiet little place. Even quieter since they closed the nightclub that once brought it so much attention. Having slept badly, Leo was feeling down. He decided to catch the bus, have his breakfast in a café then go to the readers group.

By nine, the day still didn't look as if it were ready for spring. At the bus stop there was a young man, tanned, not very tall. Despite the cold, he was only wearing a tank top that showed off his striking tribal tattoos.

'Aren't you freezing?' asked Leo.

'Yeh, a little. I daren't go and grab something warmer and miss another bus, I can't be late for work.'

'Work, eh? What a pain.'

'It's got to be done.'

'Where you from?'

'Peru.' A taxi pulls up in the bus stop and a blonde woman gets out. 'Yep, that's what we're here for. Even though I'll arrive late I can't afford a taxi.'

Leo says, 'But that driver wishes you could. That's the way of the world, you spend and we'd all be better off – the economy, I mean – though none of it trickles down to us of course.'

'And my family work fourteen hours a day just to eat…'

'To eat you've got to take whatever work you get.

94

Although I couldn't be a taxi driver, too risky these days.'

'I hear stories, but don't know what to believe.'

'There's a grain of truth in all of them, young man. They're distorted in the telling, they become urban legends.'

'In my country the people believe all those stories.'

'Folk need to believe in something.'

'They should believe in reality.'

'Truth or reality, who knows. I like to make up stories, and share them.'

'I believe in reality and my reality is the chickens I have to sex today to earn more than my compañeros. I believe in survival.'

The bus arrived and the sky seemed to close in even more, the light disappearing behind grey cloud. Leo decided to return and arm himself with his umbrella. As the Peruvian got on the bus, Leo shouted after him, 'You'll realise one day which of the two realities is false.'

4.

Leo left the house and put up his umbrella. More rain. He huddled under the shelter waiting for the bus. After a ten minute ride he was in Morley town centre – his reading group met in the library. Leo first started going simply to pass time. The books they read were commercial bestsellers with racy plots and little substance, but with Benjamin as coordinator the quality improved, new members joined too. Benjamin was from the Leeds Jewish community and studied the Cabala and spiritualism. Leo and Benjamin had many deep conversations and, although they disagreed over many things, they learnt from each other, their knowledge often overlapping.

Since he had met Leo, Benjamin had become more interested in philosophy. The book the group had chosen the previous week was Queer by William S. Burroughs. Bill Lee, the author's alter-ego, goes on a search for ayahuasca which takes him and his young lover deep into the equatorial rain forest. Lee was after the mental properties the hallucinogenic offered, like telepathy, a means of total control. Unrequited love underlay the story. For Burroughs, as for Benjamin, and for Leo, love generates the most powerful energy in the world, the most moving force, the only thing that can change fate. The will of a person in love has an energy that can't be found anywhere else. Without love, a human being is a metaphysical weakling, but the instant one loves one becomes a power of nature, liberated by a force that can last until the end of time.

Being in love was a feeling from long ago. Leo had given love in many ways, but now it was more akin to philanthropy, his concern for nature, his good deeds, generosity to those less fortunate than himself. But deep down he wanted to burn, he wanted to experience passion spent. He knew he was running out of time, because at his age things worked differently – there was nothing he could do to find the person to complete his life with. She would find him.

This week's book talk had been poor. Queer, though a short book, was a long rant that no one understood enough to read between the lines. Of the eight people there, only Benjamin and Leo brought anything to the discussion. No one could agree on a title for the following week. Out of the eight proposals they had to agree on two.

They rejected Lolita because five of the group had read

it, they threw out Island because they'd chosen another Huxley, Brave New World, only two weeks before, Death in Venice was dismissed because most of them had seen the film, Foucault's Pendulum got the chop because someone thought it was a historical novel, and Tropic of Capricorn went because they had read the other tropic a previous week. Ulysses? Too complex. They ended up voting between Hemingway's A Farewell to Arms and Dostoyevsky's Crime and Punishment. Leo proposed the American, Benjamin the Russian. The size of Crime and Punishment led the majority to vote for Hemingway.

Benjamin wasn't impressed. 'OK. A Farewell to Arms is book of the week. But always remember this, especially you,' he said, looking at Leo, 'Hemingway is nothing more than an apprentice to the master.'

Leo could tell Benjamin was irritated, making an absurd performance out of his cultural competitiveness. What are you scared of, Benjamin?

He was a manipulative type – he liked to work out the psychology of people so he could control them. During the discussion on ayahuasca, he had said he would have liked to try some, to see whether it really could put you in the minds of others. Leo imagined him controlling the members of the reading club. If he had been able to, then Hemingway would definitely not have been the choice of the week.

Benjamin was a writer. A third-rate writer, but published quite regularly and known in the region. Leo also wrote from time to time: short stories, thoughts, dialogue, conversations, chaotically composed on scraps of paper he kept loose and disorganised. Work that would possibly never see the light of day, but kept his spirits up. For him, writing was a mystical process, uplifting, touching the divine. He had a theory that it was because of this that so many writers saw themselves as inspired, touched by some celestial magic. Especially Benjamin. But Leo was relaxed. He knew that time put everyone in their place and that sooner or later time would catch up with Benjamin and expose his pretensions.

Clutching his copy of A Farewell to Arms, Leo got ready to catch the bus home. It had stopped raining and he felt hyperactive, excitable, full of power. He decided to go in the other direction and caught a bus into the centre of Leeds. During the journey he read a few pages. Of course, Hemingway couldn't touch the genius of Dostoyevsky but, for once, Leo had left with his choice of book. He felt complete – for one day he was ready to behave like the primitive western man. After all, maybe it was the only way he was going to get what he was searching for.

5.

The 221 stopped on The Headrow, opposite Leeds Library next to the Town Hall, in the centre of the city near the large open space where people meet and hang out. When England play important games they're shown on the big screen in Millennium Square. Thousands of fans flock to share the victories and defeats of the national team. Mostly defeats.

Leo went in the front entrance of the library. He was looking for an edition of a book printed in 1212, Liber Abaci, by the Italian mathematician Fibonacci. He had seen a lot about a series of numbers known as the Fibonacci sequence, but had not read the original.

The library only had one lift and the shallow steps of the magnificent stairs always tired him, so he used one of the computers on the ground floor. He could not find what he was looking for, only the famous Fibonacci Quarterly, but he had already read that twice. A nice woman about his age came over just as he was about to leave his terminal. Leo let his imagination play for a fraction of a second, imagined her when she was thirty, she must have been beautiful.

'Excuse me sir, do you know how these work?' she asked.

'Well, you could say I am learning,' answered Leo, enchanted.

'I am only looking for two books, but that grumpy woman at the counter all but called me an idiot for asking her.'

'Don't worry, I can help you. What are you looking for?'

'One by Joseph Stiglitz and another by Stanislavski.'

'Do you have a particular title ma'am?'

'No, I just want something about economics and I heard him mentioned on the radio, and I want something on acting too.'

'Good. Would you be so kind as to spell the surnames for me please?'

Leo had a feeling. In just these few seconds he sensed some kind of chemistry between them. Maybe she did too. Yes, maybe she was the woman he was waiting for, the woman destiny owed him. But if everything was preordained, should he force the situation or let it evolve naturally?

'So, economics and theatre, eh? What different worlds.'

'I'm not so sure, Mr...'

'Carragher, but call me Leo.'

'As I was going to say, Mr Leo, maybe they have a lot in common.'

'Yes, yes, certainly. I love the theatre. In fact, I work in the theatre. Would you like to come with me one day?'

The woman seemed stunned. Frozen to the spot. Like she didn't know how to respond.

'Well, lovely, yes… we must talk about it… I come here a lot… you know?' she managed to stutter nervously. 'I will see you around, I have to go…'

Definitely, this was not the one. Maybe 'the one' did not exist. Perhaps he was mistaken. All his existential theories, his labour of so many years, all wrong.

'I am sorry, madam, I did not mean to be so blunt,' he called after her as she fled.

As you approach the end of your natural life you begin looking for answers, and Leo wanted to know what was going to happen to his soul. It was clear that his body's time was nearly up, but he hoped his soul would endure, so looked out for whatever might make it complete for immortality. The yin and yang, the complete circle, a spiral in which time only expands as it unwinds, events repeating themselves incrementally, like mathematical formulae. We can't change time, time exists only to hold everything that happens inside itself – but possibly the conversation with that woman, whose name he didn't even ask, might have happened before. Not between the two of them, but it might have happened differently, or the man might also have been rejected just like him.

Reflecting on all this, he walked out into the street,

head down. It was raining. Anti-terror officers were lifting all the manhole covers and checking every corner of the city. In ten days' time the G20 summit was being held in London. All over the country they were trying to prevent protests by the increasingly militarised anti-globalisation groups. Some of them, like the Black Block, functioned as urban guerrillas and took every opportunity to attack the police as had happened in Genoa a couple of years before. Though he supported such groups ideologically, seeing them as a resistance movement, Leo hated violence.

He had always thought the global economic system was the cancer of the western world. There was simply not enough money to make it work for everybody. The crisis was no more than a symptom of the disease. Margaret Thatcher conceived a plan that changed the face of our societies. Reagan provided the muscle. The crafty, the greedy and the unscrupulous fuelled their conspiracy. But then things got out of hand. They over-speculated. Right smack in the middle of the Bush era the system froze, making its own judgement on all the injustices committed.

At the beginning of 2007, Leo Carragher predicted the collapse of the international financial system using his spatial-temporal calculations. According to Leo, economic liberalism established itself through an ever-repeated pattern. The liberal system is a circle in which everything depends on everything else. If the banks do not offer credit, people can only spend the money they actually have but want to keep hold of, so they save. Consumption dips, so prices fall, which impacts on businesses who lay off workers, so unemployment increases, and so on.

Capitalism feeds on capitalism. Engorged with greed and

avarice, it eats itself alive, as happened in 2008. It is a monster that must be controlled – we know it will react, and that reaction will be extreme, but we don't know – or don't want to know – when. Leo called it. One of his equations led him to a point in the spiral, the world economic and financial crisis in 2008. From then on the poor became the middle class and the middle class got poorer. Governments bought chips to enter the financial game. Tax havens hid themselves on islands without co-ordinates. The banks got scared of falling into protectionism. And, all the while, Thatcher continued to sip her scotch. Perhaps, through this natural economic revolution the world became more just, a natural rebalancing, an action of the golden bough. Perhaps not.

Leo did not need mathematical equations to see things coming, but what he did not see coming was what happened at the West Yorkshire Playhouse in Leeds on the 21st March 2009. There he was reprieved, given his compensation for so much suffering. He lived through an explosion.

6.

Brits tend to eat lunch at midday – something light to go on top of the breakfast they had first thing. Leo often had a homemade pasty. The ones from the chains were too fatty, but grilled vegetable was his usual choice. Back at home, he began to feel sad as he chopped, added salt but no dressing. He wished he could share his late lunch with someone. With that angel he met in the library maybe. Someone around his age, who worried about economics but enjoyed the theatre. That day's performance of The Death of Margaret Thatcher began at seven forty-five, Leo had to be there at seven. After a rest, a shower, a few poems by Baudelaire and a sandwich he set off to the Playhouse.

Forty-five minutes after Leo started work everyone was safely in their seats. Lights down, the play about to begin. Leo turned off his torch and stood next to his exit ready to watch the performance. The stage lit up.

An explosion stopped time.

Leo was blown unconscious.

He came round to see two policemen talking to him, but wanted them to shut up so he could remember his dream: she had come from over by the exit, the woman from the library, trying to get his attention. She had apologised for the way she reacted, said she would be delighted to go to the theatre with him. Surprised, Leo offered his apologies for not having asked her name. The woman smiled and whispered into his ear, Juliette.

The paramedics confirmed that he was in a stable condition and told him that, as the hospitals were overwhelmed, he would be examined by a mobile unit. Leo, now completely conscious, knew none of the audience from the stalls could have survived the explosion. Juliette. The name rang round his head.

The explosion had blown bodies apart. It was total chaos. An indoor Big Bang. As the police began to question him, he panicked. What had happened to her, to Juliette? He needed to know if she was here. Maybe the police could help him – surely they had a list of all the people who'd been in the building when the explosion occurred, but, what if she is not called Juliette? He didn't know her real name, only the one she told him in his dream.

'Mr Carragher, Leo, in the hour before you opened the doors, did you see anyone suspicious come in, anyone who shouldn't have been here?'

Leo was dazed, ears ringing. The only thought in his head was finding Juliette.

'Juliette, a tall woman with grey hair, once she was very beautiful, have you seen her? Please, I need to know. Have you seen a Juliette?'

'Calm down, Leo,' said the policeman, 'we're working on it, we'll have a list of who booked tickets as soon as we can.'

'I'll ask you the question again, Mr Carragher,' the other one said aggressively, like he was playing the bad cop to his kinder partner.

'I don't know sir, I don't know. I didn't see anything strange, nothing out of the ordinary, I don't remember anything. Let me go to the stalls, I'll help you later.'

'Mr Carragher, we have an extremely urgent situation here and very little time. No one is going downstairs, the medics and fire services are down there. Are you going to help us or not?'

'But I don't know anything, I told you, I saw nothing strange. I heard the explosion... I don't remember more, there's nothing else I can tell you.'

'He's told us all he can,' said the kind cop. 'He's out of it, he can't remember anything, we'll get more out of him tomorrow, we know bugger all ourselves now.'

'Fine, we'll talk tomorrow,' said the angry cop, already heading for the stairs.

'Leo, they are identifying the bodies out in the foyer,' the kind cop said, touching his shoulder. 'If you want to find a colleague or this Juliette you asked about, come with me. But please, keep calm, or they'll throw you out.'

7.

Doing up his shirt Leo looked around for the shoe he had lost in the explosion. Once he had put it on he limped gingerly after the young PC. If Juliette was in the theatre then she was probably dead.

'Cheer up, Mr Carragher, I'm sure this Juliette you're looking for is fine.'

'What's your name?'

'Will.'

'You know, Will, knowing a name is important, suggestive don't you think? Lolita – what does that suggest?'

'Jailbait fancied by older men.'

'That's Nabokov's doing, his Lolita.'

'Yes, very interesting, Mr Carragher, I'd not thought about it. Why are you thinking about this now, amongst all this?'

'Look, I have a confession to make.'

Leo stopped the policeman, putting a hand on his arm and looking him straight in the eye.

'Mr Carragher…'

'I don't know if the person I am looking for is called Juliette. I dreamed she was called Juliette so I can't be sure.'

'OK?' said Will as he pushed Leo on. 'I am sure you'll recognise her.'

'Yes.'

'And you are sure she was in the theatre?'

'No,' answered Leo.

'OK, nearly there. That corner is where we are bringing the bodies we can't identify. It's a madhouse, procedure is shot. But I'll show you the list of the female names we have so far. Come with me.'

The air smelt of gas and death. Blood and burnt hair. Destruction. You come all relaxed for an enjoyable evening at the theatre and – boom – you're reduced to pieces of dead meat, charred, ready to eat. Leo saw meat for all palates: well done, medium and rare, life nothing more than a black joke, but one that made him want to live. Rather than distance himself from death, he wanted to throw himself into life, to laugh at the world.

Marx said we want to live life distanced from reality by the opium of the people. Some take drugs and medication, others escape to the countryside, others practice extreme sports. For Leo, personal freedom meant not falling for a false paradise but believing in himself and his relationship with other people, believing in human values rather than a philosophy or religion, though none of this had prepared him for what had just happened in his workplace.

The list of the dead was like any other list – old class mates, exam results, or voters on the electoral roll. Surnames, first names. But, in this case, no one was going to shout, Here!

'We don't have a Juliette on the list, Mr Carragher. Does that make you feel better?'

'I don't know, she could still be inside.'

'Look, I must go, but if you want to sit down here and wait for news, I'll let you know if I find anything out.'

Another body was carried from the place of the living to the place of the dead, both legs gone, a metal object lodged in the stomach. A sight both beautiful and terrifying. There was something in the guy's expression that suggested he had died in hope. His face was intact, his nose bandaged, but obviously before the explosion. Apart from that, just a few splashes of blood across his smile. He looked Mediterranean. Not Greek, thought Leo, his forehead wasn't Italian, nor his head Portuguese. Spanish maybe.

'Alvarez, Francisco Jose Alvarez,' shouted one of the medics. 'He has Spanish ID on him.'

Leo felt a strange satisfaction. He had guessed the nationality of the corpse. Francisco Jose had died hopeful. What had brought him to the theatre? Had he come alone? What had brought him to England when he could be living in a paradise like Spain? Leo couldn't help creating a backstory for him, this was predestined: if he had not died in the theatre he would have died in a car crash or suffered some raging cancer. Leo had to believe this, he had to think that all that had happened meant something. Perhaps a medium could still contact the Spaniard's soul, detect an energy left as he passed through Leeds, through the world? Jose Francisco remained in everything he had touched, everything he left behind, even in Leo sitting beside his body.

But what about Juliette?

Two more unidentified bodies arrived. Two women. Unlike the Spanish, the English do not carry identity cards, it's something they have never wanted. Idealism over practicality. It could be ages before somebody identifies these people, Leo thought.

He wasn't a smoker but sometimes, when he was anxious, he dreamt that he was. He wanted a cigarette now. Whenever his natural equilibrium failed him, tobacco was the first thing he craved.

The body of a grey haired woman arrived. She could have been in her sixties. He got up unsteadily, banged into the table where the lists were, knocking papers to the floor. Without looking back he lunged at the stretcher and shouted, 'Juliette.'

A man in a high-vis vest took his arm. 'If you don't calm down I'll have to ask you to leave, understood?'

One of the stretcher bearers called over to the desk, 'Iliescu. Irina Iliescu.'

Leo went back and slumped in his seat. He looked at the fallen papers but hadn't the strength even to offer to pick them up. It was all too much. Maybe he should just go home.

8.

There have been a few actors who have died on stage, but until now Leo had known of only one; Moliere. Moliere and his myth. The cause of his death has never been clear and the French revolution added a touch of romance. For Leo, the death of the actor lying on the stretcher before him had the same significance as the great French playwright, who died, paradoxically, while acting in The Hypochondriac. Charles A Jones was the name to which this now lifeless body had answered for more than fifty years. Maybe he had been a little bit of a hypochondriac, like Moliere. Or maybe not, but both shared the same destiny – to die on stage.

A stretcher bearer called out. 'Ramos, he's got a Colombian passport on him, Andres Ramos.'

Leo thought. Colombia, Mexico, a life isn't worth much over there. For a few pesos any old hitman would blow your life away. No respect. Not even women and children unlucky enough to be in the target zone. No scruples. Shootings were the most normal thing in the world, like robbing candy from a supermarket, child's play. Ramos must have left Colombia to escape the violence, crossed over to the States, arrived in the UK hoping for nothing more than a proper job and to make a little money and to die an old man.

Another rescue worker called out, his voice a mezzo soprano, 'He's got a train ticket, Morley return.'

His high pitch woke Leo from his daydreams. A Colombian who worked in Morley? Could he be the lad at the bus stop this morning?

Forgetting he had been told off just a few moments earlier, Leo got up to have a look at him. The lad that morning was Peruvian, not Colombian. But Leo was curious. Maybe they knew each other, maybe they were part of the same Latino community.

'Ramtin!' shouted the rescue worker again, in his high voice, 'Ramtin, first name no surname.'

A severe woman doctor confirming the dead asked, 'Any papers to verify that, Miss Gainsborough?'

'None, doc, it's written on his shirt.'

'The shirt could be someone else's, he could have borrowed it, Miss Gainsborough,' snapped the Doctor. 'Is your sister going to come and help us or not? I'm up to here with this, we need help.'

'Yes Doctor, Lilly is on her way.'

Leo sat up quick. So many connections, he was starting to get excited. 'Lilly Gainsborough? Are you Richard Gainsborough's daughter?'

'Yes, I'm the stupid one. Help me put this stretcher over there please.'

'Your sister's the doctor in the home where I used to attend a writing workshop. She's really something special.'

'You don't say! Come on, help me over there with this.'

Leo picked up the stretcher in an almost hallucinogenic state. A tiny window opened in his cerebral cortex and his psyche merged with everything around him, inducing a weird state through which he moved very slowly. Had he been driving he would have had an accident. Not stopping quickly enough, he bashed into the wall, caused one of Ramtin's arms to fall and hang from the stretcher. A little notebook fell on the floor.

'Be careful!' shouted the doctor.

It was a small notebook with yellow pages. On the cover was written LS6 and the name Ramtin. The Doctor was wrong, he wasn't wearing borrowed clothes. Leo opened the notebook, finding an address on the last page. LS6 Bar, 16A Headingley Lane, LS6 2AS. He slipped the notebook into his pocket and stood up again.

Lilly arrived. She was a stunner, a draw-dropping blonde, not young anymore, carrying a little flesh, but people still stared at her. The air crackling around her gave Leo goose bumps. Something strange was going on. Everything that could possibly happen was happening at the same time. There had to be a reason, a purpose. Lilly looked worried. Leo stayed in his seat, didn't greet her. He had always

114

thought there was something about her. Although she chatted pleasantly enough, she had a dangerous negative energy which Leo knew could drive any man to ruin. When he had met her at the home he suspected a drug problem. Why else would her busy businessman father always be dropping in if not to keep an eye on her?

She grabbed a gown, snapped on latex gloves and, unconcerned whether she put the other doctor's nose out of joint, Lilly took charge of the area where the bodies were arriving. Leo could see her face was beginning to show the first signs of age – slack skin, bags around her eyes. Beauty creams can patch up some areas, but the throat never lies. Suddenly, her face turned even whiter than it had been. It crumpled, distorted. Her eyes filled with terror. It became obvious she knew one of the dead, no, two of the dead. The Spaniard and the Colombian. Overcome by hysteria, she pulled the stretchers with the two bodies together and knelt between them, an arm over each. The image too theatrical, her head down, tears falling to the floor. She screamed. The all-powerful doctor, breaker of so many hearts, herself broken.

9.

The bodies kept arriving and the emergency workers couldn't cope. Leo put up no resistance when they asked him to leave the area. He felt any chance of finding Juliette was fading, maybe she had not been there. He wanted to smoke. As the shock began to wear off Leo began to think clearly again, to realise exactly what had happened. He wanted to cry, to shout out. Since he came round from the explosion, since he talked to the policemen, he had been dreaming. Juliette, or whatever she was called, was not there. She had no reason to be there. It was his mind playing tricks.

He went down to the street. Fresh air replaced the smell

of fire, of burnt flesh. He walked into the cigarette cloud of a young girl standing outside looking worried. Maybe the loved one she had been searching for was still missing. He could not help but ask.

'Are you OK?'

She did not reply.

'Are you looking for someone too?'

The girl, looked down, fighting back tears, then nodded.

'Can I help you?'

Leo could hardly hear her say, 'One of the actors.'

Leo knew none of the actors had survived.

'Some members of the cast are OK,' he said to console her.

A looming shape blocked out the street light.

'Marisa! Where is Little Fi? Do you know anything? Marisa?'

Leo stepped back and watched an enormous guy come between him and Marisa and struggled to place the language she replied in.

'Naõ so, Carlos, ainda naõ.'

Leo backed away from the scene. He imagined them together, their friendship, closeness, commitment. How Marisa was in love with her actor, Little Fi. Although Leo was still looking for love, he enjoyed seeing others luckier than himself. Seeing Marisa and the giant Carlos, answers came into his mind before his head thought of the questions, doors opened without keys. Leo didn't think, he felt happy with the simple certainty that he was alive, in the world, in this street, under the glare of these street lamps. Breathing fresh air while smoking a cigarette is as contradictory as it is necessary, because life is imperfection. The theatre had exploded together with the world. They each explode every day.

10.

I have just died, thought Leo, I am part of all this: Marisa and Carlos, Lilly, the Spaniard and the Colombian. I don't know if life is going to give me everything it owes me, and I don't know if I will get to heaven. If I don't find my other half, I only hope that some soul somewhere will let me help them.

He cried out, 'Please, Little Fi, Show up!'

Suddenly Marisa and Carlos rushed over to a stretcher being put into an ambulance and Leo realised that Little Fi was not that little. They were talking about that Filipe, big Filipe, the actor in the play. Big Carlos hurled himself at the stretcher and one of the auxiliaries shooed him away. Filipe gave them the thumbs up and everyone calmed down. Leo was glad that Filipe had survived, he was good guy if a little lost in the real world. Maybe this girl, Marisa, would be able to sort him out. As Fi was put in the ambulance, Marisa and Carlos hugged, and Leo smiled for them. Now it really was time to go home.

With the smoke, the flashing blue lights and sirens, it felt like a film set. Leo left the scene like an actor lamenting his lowly status in the cast. He ached. The world which he would have liked to enjoy did not need him. He ached more than anybody. Still he had not asked why. He wanted to leave the scene and wake up hours later to discover it had all been a dream, that none of his work colleagues were dead. He just wanted to be given a button to press, to turn off, reformat, wipe and begin the day again.

Then Juliette was there. Alive. Walking with a man. By the crossing on The Headrow they stopped and faced each other. They held hands, then hugged, then a kiss on the cheek. Leo breathed a sigh of relief and through the sound of pumps and engines saw her lips mouth, 'Don't worry, I'm okay. Bye, Steven, take care.'

Leo rushed over and without greeting or introduction said, 'Madam, are you alright, are you hurt?'

She turned, a bit wobbly on her feet, surprised to see him.

Leo ploughed on, 'Do you remember me from the library?'

Her face lit up. It was her, his angel, open-eyed. 'Mr Carragher!'

'You recognise me!'

'Mr Carragher, believe me – sorry I am confused, what

just happened there? Was it a bomb?'

He replied, but his answer was drowned out by the siren of a passing fire engine.

She picked a fleck of plaster from his beard.

'I've spent all day thinking about our meeting at the library. What a fool I was, like a silly teenager.'

Leo could not believe what he was hearing. Now he had no need of mathematical formulae. He hoped it wasn't just the shock that was making his angel talk this way.

'Mr Carragher, you don't know how much I have been hoping I would meet you again, even if just to apologise for not speaking or telling you my name...'

'Juliette, isn't it?'

'Julianne, I am Julianne.'

'Oh, a tiny error!' shouted Leo, full of sudden joy.

'Excuse me, Mr Carragher?'

'Leo, call me Leo. Um, I hope it would not alarm you if I asked... if you would allow me to walk you home.'

'No, of course not. I won't make the same mistake as this morning. But I live quite far away.'

'Tell me.'

'Headingley, LS6.'

'Perfect.'

'You live there too?'

'No but there is a café there called LS6, where I think we'll find all our beginnings and the end of everything!'

LS4

1.

The girl lying next to him asked, Isn't today the first day of spring?

Filipe couldn't remember her name. The alarm clock read 09.00 – 21.03.09.

It had been a long night. An explosive cocktail of running into his ex, a fight with a bunch of English louts, flirting with a girl from work, and finally fucking this nameless girl he knew only as his ballet teacher's squeeze.

A hundred needles stuck in his eyes. Beer. Too much beer bloated his stomach, blocked his brain, made him want to piss all the time and turned him into a drunk. He hated ending up in this mess.

He looked in the mirror. One eye was swollen. He didn't remember it being like that when he arrived home. He didn't remember going to bed. Even worse; he couldn't remember the name of the girl lying next to him.

He looked at her again, searching for inspiration, a name he could associate with her face and those gorgeous tits. Nothing. It was something Latin, like that Hispanic actress, but would not come. His more immediate problem was the etiquette of getting her out of his house. Maybe he could fuck her again before getting rid of her, she had breasts to die for, but he was not drunk and was beginning to tire of screwing bodies without names. Just pieces of meat – cute, yet impersonal pussy. Filipe was beginning to need something more. He wanted to know what it was like to make love when you were in love, when a couple felt what they were doing was physical consummation of shared feelings, not just satisfying primal animal instinct. Now thirty-three, Filipe was beginning to tire of his success as a performer, something was missing, something beyond the pure banality and frivolity of these flings and the total lack of communication. It was destroying what little belief he had in his ability to love.

He turned to look in the mirror again, the swelling seemed to be getting worse.

In the evening he had to work but a good make-up job and the lights would cover up the black eye. Being an actor was never easy. However tired or broken you might be, you had to wear the right face for the role. He wasn't really an actor yet anyway, more of a dancer. He had danced since he was very small, first in his homeland Angola and later in Portugal, his point of entry into Europe. After tasting the success and pleasures of a dancer's life he had decided to develop his career and threw himself into acting. Soon afterwards he was cast in a small touring role in The Death of Margaret Thatcher. He was enjoying his new adventure. What he didn't like was the lifestyle. Every night after the show the cast would go out partying. Beautiful women, VIP treatment, casual sex, drugs… throughout his stay in the UK he had lived the life many starry-eyed kids could only dream of. Now he felt empty, fragile, as if the smallest puff of wind would carry him away. He was looking for something more. He needed to know what love was as soon as possible. With a woman, preferably. Men didn't attract him, but then again, sex was sex.

He went to the bathroom and got ready to rid himself of the stubble that had grown since the day before. His part obliged him to shave every day. Cesaria Evora began to sing – it was the girl's mobile. Naked, he went back to the bedroom but stopped, he still didn't know her name. She was gorgeous. He remembered that she was a hairdresser, but that was the only thing he knew. The girl struggled to open her eyes and rolled across the bed to find her phone. Filipe could hear the voice at the other end shouting her name: Marisa! She was called Marisa. He remembered how all the night before he had been calling her Marisa Tomei, after the actress.

The voice on the other end of the line sounded very angry. They spoke in Portuguese, Portuguese with a Cape Verdean accent. Marisa said she was sorry, she had slept in and would be there in less than fifteen minutes. She jumped out of bed shouting, 'Shit! Fuck! Fuck! Fuck! You let me sleep in.'

'Where do you work darling?'

'Salon, Albion Street.'

'It won't take long to get there.'

'I need a shower to wake up, I stink of drink. You mind?'

'No, of course not, eh, Marisa, darling…'

'Ah, I see you've learnt my name.'

This blunt Cape Verdean was growing on him. Maybe she was what he had been looking for.

'Marisa, honey, do you fancy coming to see my play tonight?'

'No, I hate theatre. It depresses me, it's all lies. I need reality, not something to take me away from it.'

Filipe got into the shower with her and they made love. At least, for Filipe what they made in the shower was love.

Dressed, she dashed out and he waved goodbye to her from the window. As he turned to go back into the bathroom he saw that she had left her mobile on the bed.

2.

After all these years he had grown accustomed to Europe and his memories of Africa became fainter every day. Sometimes, though, he thought of his family and his childhood in Luanda. The sea, the port, the streets packed with people. When Filipe was born the war had already started. He knew nothing of the conflict. Not the fall of Portuguese rule, nor the Carnation Revolution, nor the involvement in his country's war of Cuba, the Soviet Union, the USA and South Africa. But he knew the deadly price his continent paid when the colonisers decided to abandon them to their fate. Any state undergoes a period of transition when the government changes, but the African countries began from scratch without the necessary resources. The Belgians abandoned the Congo, leaving a nation arbitrarily defined by lines on a map in which four hundred distinct ethnic groups lived. Bringing together so many different cultures was only possible with the most drastic of systems: dictatorship. Mobutu created a feeling of national unity at the cost of a handful of conflicts that are still not settled. European wars, although they may be long, like in the Balkans, end with international intervention. But Africans aren't a threat to the strong, and nobody wants to mediate in their conflicts. Like so many places, Africa was a testing ground for the Cold War, but neither NATO nor the UN had the guts to get involved in Rwanda when the Hutu decided to exterminate the entire Tutsi population. It didn't interest them. Little more than three hundred blue helmets were sent to try and avert genocide. That's all. A conflict of visceral hatred once again spilled over into the Congo where the conflict still trudges on in what has been called Africa's World War. Coltan, diamonds, petroleum. Any resource is good and cheap for the western multi-nationals, who operate in their own interests and place little value on the lives of Africans.

At the beginning of the nineties, when Filipe was thirteen, he and his father emigrated to Portugal, which had just joined the EU. The streets of Lisbon were full of people from the old colonies, Mozambique, Cape Verde, Angola, Guinea. It was there that he met Carlos, a huge black chef who worked in a Spanish restaurant in Alfama.

One night, while walking the streets of his neighbourhood looking for work in any restaurant who'd employ a thirteen year old illegal, Carlos crossed his path. Filipe only used the alleys running behind everything, and in one of them a gang of Angolans attacked him even though they knew he had no money. Instead of robbing him they threw him to the ground and gave him a few good kicks in the kidneys. Filipe was so terrified that he shat himself without even realising it. He thought that he was going to die. At that moment, Carlos Dos Santos, an enormous Angolan, came out to throw his kitchen waste into the alley and saw what was happening. Though it was a humid Lisbon evening the ground felt cold to little Filipe. But Carlos was hot, all fired up. Filipe heard, Get off my brother! before watching the kind of fight you only saw in films.

'Are you looking for work, irmaõ?'

'Yes but I'm too young.'

'You could work here all the hours you want little one, but black money, then everyone is happy, OK?'

That night, after Carlos became his godfather, and gave him his nickname, Little Fi never felt lonely again. Months later, Carlos, all his siblings and their mother decided to emigrate to England in search of higher wages. Portugal had work but no money. Carlos left a note: Little Fi, right now you can't come with us, but I promise that I will write to you soon and tell you how and when you can join us. It felt like what he was really saying was, Goodbye. Fi would remain alone in Lisbon, without the protection of the Dos Santos. They had been much more of a family to him than his own father, who had upped sticks to Oporto to move in with a girlfriend and only sent him the occasional miserly cheque. In the homeless shelter he had a roof to sleep under, at least until he was sixteen, but he hated the food and missed the Dos Santos family.

As time passed, Fi realised that Carlos was not only generous, but stuck to his word. Six months later a letter arrived telling Little Fi to be patient, giving him an address and saying that in four or five months Carlos would be returning to Portugal for his maternal aunt, who had been widowed. And that is what happened.

Travelling from Lisbon to Santander was his introduction into the rest of Europe and the rest of his life. After a long train journey which reminded him of the westerns he had watched on RTP on Saturday afternoons, Little Fi crossed a new frontier into Spain. The carriage was divided into compartments housing between six and eight people and all their luggage. In the middle of the night the train stopped somewhere on the Spanish border. Pampillosa. There, they had to wait for more than four hours for another train to Salamanca. It was freezing.

It took a week to get from Salamanca to Santander. Carlos' aunt fell ill and was admitted to a hospital in Zamora, where they slept and ate for free for a few days, before crossing to the UK. Since then, Carlos and the Dos Santos had been the only family that mattered to him.

3.

There is a large black community in Leeds. Some come from the old British colonies, especially Zimbabwe, but also many people from Botswana, Malawi, Zambia and Ghana, not forgetting the Caribbean pioneers. Chapeltown, the area with the biggest black population, rises up a hill to the north east of the city from which you can look back and see the whole of Leeds. The low redbrick houses seem to stretch for miles around in an endless sprawl. It is said the urban corridor stretches as far as Manchester.

Leeds developed with the wool trade and expanded rapidly during the middle of the 19th century, swallowing surrounding towns and villages like Morley. The construction of the Leeds-Liverpool canal and the arrival of the railway led to an industrial explosion that created the metropolis of nearly 800,000 people it is today. Leeds became a modern city quickly adapting to the challenges of development. In 1928 it became the first place in the world to install automatic traffic lights and, more recently, the first place to have total broadband coverage. No tourists come to Leeds. Business, college, shopping, services… anything fleeting or fast-moving. But it's also a city that you get to know slowly, a city you fall in love with. In the centre there are red brick buildings with external fire escapes that remind you of Boston, there's a business district, a huge enclave of meetings and events, there's the canal and the river, museums and parks, it has life. A walk along the river path by the Aire, or an afternoon shopping in the pedestrian area. A good city to be in, a city where many paths cross.

Chapeltown is postal district LS7, but Filipe preferred LS6 because there was more alternative culture, more house parties, students, different ethnicities, more indie shops, more weed… but above all, it was a district that felt more like other European cities, everything mixed up together. Many of the residential streets also housed businesses, making it different to other areas, which were either business or residential.

When they first arrived in Leeds, Carlos and Filipe lived in Beeston in the south. Generally the southern areas were poorer than those in the north. Or used to be, things were changing. They quickly moved to Chapeltown where they felt more comfortable among their own. Beeston was a ball-ache, it felt like a nowhere place, just a main road lined with houses. There was a stretch with pubs, shops, a supermarket and a bookies, but the only distinguishing feature of the area was Elland Road stadium. Match days were the highlight of the week.

One of those match days, back in 1994, Filipe and Carlos were watching a game. At half time, an announcement asked for young volunteers to take part in an improvised dance piece on the pitch. Filipe got chosen to perform the most athletic part. Two somersaults and a corkscrew with a good landing were enough to have him selected by the choreographer for a trial in his dance company. Leeds United won that day, thanks to two goals by Thomas Brolin, but the real hero wasn't Scandinavian, he was Angolan, and he was ready to sacrifice everything to make the most of this, the opportunity of a lifetime.

Tough training, tears, falls, low self-esteem, Little Fi put up with all this during his adolescence. The training was hard and each time the challenge bigger. He had no time for anything else, only for training, for dance, for success. No time for friends, video games, football matches or girls. Little Fi was a boy made of gold, whose mentors protected him as though he were a football star. Carlos and his family were conscious of how all the effort might be damaging for the boy, but because of their ever-present financial situation they depended on his future success and supported him all the way. By the time he was nineteen, he was dancing with one of Britain's leading dance companies and touring all over Europe. He had found his place. As well as working, he now had time for going out, rubbing shoulders with important people, trying different drugs, different beds and generally making up for all those years when he had lived only for dancing.

At thirty came another moment of change. He knew that if he remained with the company he would stagnate; he had two options, music or theatre. All his life he had accepted the roles that he had been given but enjoyed the status they gave him so, not knowing anything about real life, he chose acting.

4.

Marisa Tomei – Marisa the hairdresser – had left and Filipe wanted to doze a while longer, but he couldn't drift off. His mind was full of percussion and blood. He could not remember what had happened. Last night was a blank wiped out by drink, he had lost the plot again with booze. These theatre people could get away with anything. They knew everyone – all the local managers, dealers, women up for a good time. Living in their bubble meant that life for Filipe had not been linear, he had not learnt things step by step, but discovered the world blow by blow. Recently he had come to the conclusion that getting involved with his colleagues was not a good idea. That was why he had gone for Marisa last night.

He knew what he was like as a lover. However he tried to change, quantity as well as quality was what he was after. He didn't tend to spend more than two or three nights with the same person. He avoided involvement, circled round sentiment. His only ambition was to keep his status as an actor, be the envy of his friends, and be as happy as possible. He was sensitive and vaguely remembered once having feelings for somebody, but it was already a moth-eaten memory that he preferred not to stir up. He'd been in countless orgies and had once slept with a guy who claimed to be the casting director for a Hollywood blockbuster and promised him a walk on part. But Fi didn't make the cut. He had never felt so small. Bitter. Humiliated. From then on he only went with women. He had not indulged in his favourite fantasy for some time. Most women found his size a problem, they rejected him because they just couldn't fit round him, even with lubricants. For Fi, anal sex was total subjugation, it granted him absolute power over another body from the inside, a mystical status like the Orishas. A tantric experience, complete hedonistic delight, his only goal, his constant, his end.

Marisa had dilated well. Sober now, Fi began to realise last night had been a special moment. Beyond the sex he had felt something else different. In her openness, her brown eyes, time stood still. For once he was totally in the moment, at the centre of the universe. This morning, all mixed up in bed, the rain came, clearing his mind. Everything was wonderful.

The good thing about being an actor is that you don't have to clock in early. The mornings are yours to enjoy however you like, on the PlayStation, watching TV, wasting time, going to the cinema, for a walk, lunching out… People shouldn't spend so much time cooped up in offices, clocking in, day after day, for forty years. You think about it and you console yourself with, at least I'll be done by five, it's not a difficult job, there's a good atmosphere in the office… and so what? It's an obligation, something you have to do if you want to be part of the system, and if you don't have a steady income the bills end up swallowing you whole. Filipe thought himself the most fortunate man in the world. He lived doing what he loved and tonight, for a change, he was playing in his hometown. Carlos and the others around him worked hard to pay bills, rent and buy food. The little they saved they sent to Angola. But the price Filipe had paid to get to where he wanted to be was higher than all the bills of his neighbours put together. Although he thought it had been worth it, there was still something lacking. He was carrying too much. He wanted to lose some of the baggage he lugged around with him, open up, let down the defences with which he protected himself but which also harmed him. Yet Filipe had a pathology common in modern society – he was scared to love.

The sky seemed to have calmed down enough to acknowledge the arrival of spring. He thought about going out. But he had things to do first, so decided to stay in. He wrapped himself in his sheets and was just about to drift off when his phone rang. Carlos told him he was going through a bad patch – his sister had just had another baby and each time found it more difficult to get by. Fi decided to give them a good chunk of money.

'Don't worry about paying me back, brother. Really, Carlos, you saved my life, it's the least I can do in return.'

They agreed to meet in half an hour at a Starbucks in the city centre.

By quarter to ten, Filipe and his swollen face were walking through the pedestrian area in Leeds city centre. He arrived at the coffee shop before Carlos. Weird, he was always on time. Fi hoped that nothing bad had happened. Although, thinking about it, nothing ever happened to Carlos. He was a prodigy of nature, and sure enough moments later Carlos appeared, eclipsing everybody around him.

'Si irmao, all's good. I bumped into an old workmate. A Spanish ham cutter, he worked as a waiter at my restaurant.'

'Your restaurant?'

'The restaurant where I work, irmao, you fucker.'

'Ah!'

'A nice guy but a bit weird. He was scared, I think he thought I was going to mug him, ha irmao, before he recognised me.'

5.

Carlos continued his daily search for work and Fi began to search the city centre salons for Marisa. He imagined she would be a real hairdresser, one of those women who had a whole stack of stories to keep the conversation going, a girl who could chat with anyone. He vaguely remembered her saying she worked near Albion Street. He entered the salons one by one, almost all of them franchises. The stylists interrupted their chit chat with clients while Filipe asked them if there was a Marisa working there. No sign of her. Then, as he was nearing the end of the street he turned right and saw a sign: Women's Hairdressers.

He didn't even need to go inside. He saw Marisa in the

doorway, saying goodbye to a grey haired lady. She took a cigarette from her apron pocket and Filipe reached her just in time to light it for her. She broke into a huge smile.

'Thank you, cowboy,' she said.

'You left your phone at my place.'

'Very kind.'

'Surprised?'

'I knew you'd find me.'

'I was thinking you might like to come to the theatre with me tonight after all?'

'I told you. I hate theatre.'

'But you won't hate me in mine.'

'If you hang around here I'll start hating you. I've got to get back to work.'

'You only just lit that fag. Anyone nipping out for a smoke can have five minutes.'

'I'll call you next week. My cousins from London are arriving tomorrow and I'm going to be busy with them.'

'Fine, that means that you might feel like going out for a bit tonight. A bit of air before dealing with family is always good.'

'I don't know Filipe, honestly… What time does this thing start?'

'Late enough, seven forty-five. You have no excuse.'

Marisa showed her first sign of submission since the night before and Filipe quickly took advantage.

'Here. I'll leave a ticket for you at box office. Marisa! If you feel like coming, come. If not, call me next week. OK?'

Mission accomplished, Filipe headed home. He was still tired from the night before. He fancied a little weed to drift off in front of the TV with. His regular dealer, Nino, would already be up and about.

Nino was of Hindi descent, born in England. Beneath his hard guy act screaming round in a pimped up car, he was a complete softy, and gay. One night they bumped into each other in Mint, one of Leeds' best known clubs, and Nino had given him some liquid ecstasy. The high had been so strong that Fi had lost his friends along with his awareness of space and time. When the party was over and the club had begun to empty, he found himself alone with Nino. They left together and talked for hours. There was chemistry. A pure chemistry of friendship. Filipe had been a loyal customer for a long time, but he had never spoken so in depth with his dealer. Nino told him that he had got into this dangerous line of work after he got his heart broken, but had yet to find satisfaction. Their words started to meld and then, before Fi realised, so did their mouths. The ecstasy carried them. It wasn't Fi's first time, but it was the first time that it was like this, like with a girl, little by little. They went back to Fi's place and had sex. But when Fi came down and he realised what had happened he regretted it and asked Nino to leave. Long phone calls and a few meet-ups in quiet out of the way places were enough to make things clear, that it had been a mix up, the false effect of the drug. But Nino was hooked. He gave Fi weed, sometimes pills, asked him out to parties. Filipe felt bad, it wasn't that he didn't feel anything for Nino, but the thought of him as a lover repulsed him. He was his dealer, a good person to party with. And that was it.

Thinking it over Filipe decided it was probably better not to call Nino. Although they hadn't seen each other for a while, Filipe doubted that he had got over it, as last time he had been very upset. He knew another dealer, a Spaniard called Jesus, but he was gay too and also seemed to have the hots for him. Nino inspired more confidence, even after everything that had happened...

'Nino, are you around? You couldn't bring me over some gear?'

Five minutes later Nino was knocking at the door. Fi opened up and the boy hurled himself through, trying to kiss him like a scene in a Bollywood movie – the distraught despairing lover. How could Filipe really feel something for Nino, when he couldn't even feel anything for the women he slept with? Filipe pushed him away and Nino fell back against the table. He pulled a gun from behind his back and aimed at Fi.

'Fuck me or I'll kill you.'

'Come on Nino dude, leave it, what's wrong with you ... this won't solve anything.'

Nino pointed the gun at his own head, his finger on the trigger.

'OK, I'll kill myself.'

'No, dude, don't do it. Kill me, go on, kill me. Oh, come on, just drop the gun mate, come on Nino, you silly fucker.'

Nino dropped the gun, fell to his knees and burst into sobs like a child who had come off their bike. Pathetic for a lad who acted so hard. Fi picked up the pistol. It wasn't loaded. It had been a charade, a performance, a little number Nino had orchestrated as a last resort. For the first time in ages Filipe felt bad, all this mess felt his fault. He saw Nino out to his car and left him there weeping. A sad sight.

Back in his house, a bag of weed had fallen on the floor. At least something good had come from all this. If Nino had the slightest bit of self-respect, he wouldn't try to see him again, and if Fi had the slightest bit of decency he wouldn't call him next time he needed weed. Now it was time to unwind and snooze until he had to leave for the show.

6.

Theatre is the art of telling stories to an audience using a combination of words, gestures, scenery, music and sound. You don't need to be that clever to see how in our everyday lives we behave quite theatrically. Cynically to be precise. It was one of the first lessons Filipe learnt and why he chose theatre over music as a career. Now he was beginning to make a name for himself in the theatre, he was dreaming of cinema, of Hollywood.

Rapturous applause woke him from his siesta. He had been asleep for a few hours. His mobile was ringing. His DJ friend FresCo was in town and fancied a few pints. Fi couldn't say no, but he didn't want to leave the house.

While still too early to start preparing himself, it was too late to go out. Acting required a lot of concentration. He popped out to Tesco Extra for a couple of beers and then tidied up his place.

FresCo had made his name through Bill Gainsborough, owner of several bars in the city. He had started out playing funk in some of Gainsbourgh Jr's most seedy clubs, but his persistence, determination and talent had allowed him to cut the ties that held him to the man who had gave him his break and move to London in search of something better. Little by little he was making a name for himself as one of the most sought after DJs in the country.

'Success?' Asked FresCo raising a beer can to his lips. 'I get up at 6.30 in the morning, go straight to the studio. I don't have a girlfriend, barely have a social life and I can't remember what it's like to go out at the weekend because I'm always working. OK, I am doing what I love, but I'm not sure that doing it at this level is really worth it. Look, everyone tells you, play sport, doing sport is good for you. But if you play sport at a high level you risk injury much more than you do sitting on the sofa, eh? Understand me?'

'But now you're rubbing shoulders with the best, eh?'

'The best? It depends how you define the best. Some of them have been around for so long and they haven't developed, haven't changed. Some of them haven't evolved much at all. They make a lot of money, behave like fucking divas and walk round with their retinue of whores, but they're imbeciles, no personality. OK, the best may have their bad habits, but they are the most normal, they're honest, interesting, they work hard.'

'Sure, but of course we know whether art is good or bad

depends on what the critics say. And who are these critics? Artists of No, castrated creatives who can only analyse what has happened, not something not yet made, not create it. It's their fault Van Gogh died poor, depressed and without selling a canvas. They thought he was shit. Until someone saw the light and said, Fuck, this guy's a genius, he has found a whole new way of painting!'

'Yeh, and Sotheby's rub their hands.'

'Yeh, yeh, exactly. They're all a bunch of crooks.'

'It never works logically. If you're good, nobody guarantees you a spot, if you go commercial, work with the guys who know what sells, you betray yourself, you have a year or two of glory, but it doesn't last …'

'I know what you're saying my friend. I know what you are saying but I'm going to have to leave you. I need to shower and prepare for the show.'

'Cool, I've got to go too. I promised my Dad I'd drop by, he's gone into that old folks place in Headingley.'

'Say hi to John from me, and you take care FresCo,' said Filipe giving him a hug.

He opened his tubs of cream and began to recite his part as he applied moisturiser. He had not thought about her for a while, but seeing his empty bed from the bathroom, he wondered what Marisa would decide. He hated uncertainty. He did not know whether she would come to the show. It was possible he would not know what she felt about him for a week, if she even decided to call. He wanted to do it right with this one, be honest, be a person with soul, someone who gave out positive energy. Marisa would be an investment in the future. One he was ready to change for, to leave his shitty defensiveness, step out of his armour plating and dare to love. Because he had kept all of his love hermetically sealed deep in his heart, it had not lost a gram of strength, it was intact, waiting for the moment to come out. Without doubt, this was the moment. He had never felt this close to letting go.

7.

Despite his three hour siesta, the day had been intense and Filipe felt tired. Spring fever. He got out of the shower, dried himself, recited the last and most dramatic bit of his part to the mirror, grabbed his bag and took a taxi. During the journey, The Killers song All these things I've done played in his head, he nodded along, his eyes a cinema screen showing the documentary of his life from Luanda to Great Britain where things had taken off. His success had run in parallel to Neo-liberalism. His problems too.

The West Yorkshire Playhouse was a modern building. He wondered, how many years would it last? The classic theatres stood the test of time, but new ones, like TVs or computers were more like consumables, we use them then throw them away.

Pisa Leo, the usher, the Google man, Leo Carragher, the person who knew something about everything, was leaning against the box office counter.

'Break a leg.'

'I'd prefer some luck Leo. Luck's more useful, I'm not superstitious.'

'That's OK, saying good luck won't send us all up in smoke.'

'Today is the first day of the rest of my life Leo, a girl's coming to see me who-'

'Get on you, you're always the same.'

Filipe had also had a fling with one of the cast. Despite her saddle bags, typical of Spanish women, her tight ass turned him on. He'd had some good times with her but got bored quickly, and had moved on as soon as another woman crossed his path. He looked at her perfect back. You wouldn't say she was fat, just softly padded. As usual she gave him a nasty look, trying to put him off before the show. She knew she had no chance. She wanted to leave the show but couldn't. Shooting daggers at him was all she could do now. Filipe knew and took no notice.

Beyoncé, stuck to his mirror, received him with the same smile as always. Just as he liked. Sometimes she whispered. He closed the dressing room door so he could hear her speaking, whistling, murmuring secret words only he could understand. He felt as though his world was about to explode, to change. Sometimes his life seemed crazy and he couldn't distinguish between fact and fiction, he didn't know how to deal with relationships, how to relax into a quiet life with someone who was actually worth it. Marisa and what he felt for her was the only reality he could hang on to at the moment. A reality in which Beyoncé did not talk to him because she was just a photo nothing more, and the things he could hear probably came from the plumbing, or some machine, a gas leak.

After hair and makeup he started the breathing exercises he always did before going on stage. It still wasn't his time for his cue and waiting in the wings made him nervous, he preferred not to see anything, preferred to hide from the scene and step on blindly when it was his turn, without giving himself the opportunity to anticipate anything. So as the lights went up, Filipe headed back to his dressing room.

LS5

1.

'Who's to blame for the crisis?' Asks Benjamin rhetorically. 'George Bush? The banks? Governments? Consumers? No, Ramtin my friend, the person most to blame is Alan Greenspan. It was the regulators' fault. Markets rely on control and regulation and the regulators - the central banks, the SEC, the FED didn't react in time. Markets fail because they rely on people and the regulator's job is to spot problems before it's too late. Some warned the financing of junk mortgages was irresponsible, but that kind of Madoff activity carried on. Bill Clinton, with his 'a house for everybody' policy, was all for sub primes. OK, the Bush administration pushed the whole thing to the brink, but you can't just blame the Republicans.'

I interrupted, 'It was the Chinese.' Benjamin's dogmatic theorising always annoys me. 'They lent to the Americans at low interest rates so the yuan remained stable, the dollar high and they could both produce goods at competitive prices. Everyone knew China being the new global power was out to destabilise the existing empires.'

'You're right.' Says Benjamin much to my surprise, 'China and the US have blown apart the world to create a single global economy.'

'That's it. And neoliberalism did the rest.'

'Exactly, it's the politicians who fucked up.'

'As always.'

'And useless little Europe got dragged down by the mess on the other side of the Atlantic. We've all fallen. It's always been risky, Reagan acted as if everyone was loaded, but obviously that wasn't the case. When the Chinese middle classes enter the game, my hope is that technology will be the driver and not the need for natural resources, otherwise global conflict will be inevitable.'

'Yeh, but some things never change.'

'Oh yes? Like what?'

'Like what?' Sighed Benjamin, 'Israel has been in conflict for years with no solution in sight and we all carry on as normal.'

'It can't feel very normal in Palestine, every day less land, more bodies.'

'OK, let's drop the subject, you don't know enough to be able to talk about it. Anyway, I have to get to Morley, for my reading group.'

LS6

The Jewish areas of Leeds are in the north, Roundhay and Wigtown, places Benjamin hates, preferring LS6, a more cosmopolitan part of the city. He is a clever guy, with whom I have had lots of heated conversations in the cafe and its garden, but he is too arrogant and manipulative. More than ten minutes with him and you enter the danger zone. But we do agree on the energy of LS6, particularly this cafe of the same name. It has a great atmosphere, which is why I always come here, despite Benjamin.

It's eight-thirty in the morning on the first day of spring and the sky looks hostile as usual. Ideas start coming with the first drops of rain, I leave the garden, sit inside at the bar and take out my yellow notebook to get them down. The plan is already sketched out, now I need to add the action, characters, descriptions of the city. I haven't quite got the ending yet.

For the first time in my life I am confident that I have written something good, but it will be some time yet before I know if it will be successful. I've got a meeting with an editor. My life's dream is closer than ever before, but depends on some fat guy with a moustache and toupee making a commercial decision. That's how the literary world works. I'd love to set up a publishing house to publish all the great works rejected by editors. I would have the best catalogue in the world. Losing one literary jewel is worse than losing a thousand lesser books, but it happens all the time in this industry with more plagiarists than writers and more ghost writers than a graveyard.

I work in the dark arts myself, a ghost writer. It's not a bad job for a guy with dark skin, a moustache, who wears sandals, a refugee. Last year I wrote four novels, one of them for a very successful woman sold more than twenty thousand copies, that's a lot of royalties. But I feel under-valued, my ideas never see the light as I would have them, so have no meaning for me. After a long struggle I am close to publishing my first book, the first book that is really mine. This afternoon I have a meeting with an indie publisher who is interested in a manuscript I sent him, and I am going to take the opportunity to sell him my new idea, sketched out here in my yellow notebook.

2.

Being Kurdish means belonging to an ethnic minority. It doesn't matter where you are, even in my own country, Iran, we belong to a group making up only 10 percent of the population. With the fall of the Shah and the arrival of the Islamic Republic and their opposition to the USA, I thought our time had come. But fanaticism and money are a lethal combination, the war machine of a rich country costs too much just to be left to rust. The Iran Iraq War forced me into exile - frontiers, border controls, endless roads of dust and rubble. These are the memories of my nomadic life, when all I hoped for was a counter revolution that would allow me to settle some place. I ended up in Turkey, the worst place for a Kurd. However, it was my gateway to Europe and asylum in Great Britain. I am happy here, I have been able to get on with my life, develop personally and professionally, be free. I can now say I have my life made. The only dream I have left is to publish a book with my name on the cover. It isn't for my ego, but to get a sense of justice from looking back on my journey. Life may have treated me much better than most of my fellow Kurds, but I still deserve this.

Before arriving here I spent time with relatives in France. We lived in a ghetto on the outskirts of Paris. Life there was not like here, over there the ghetto is a circle you can't break out of, it gives you protection, but at the same time limits your dreams. There was nothing beyond. Britain is different. You don't have ghettos, only neighbourhoods. Here they have set me up to be a useful member of society. Back home my academic parents' act of revolution against the mullahs was to speak English at home, so I had the language but the class gave me idiom and an insight into Anglo-Saxon culture. ESOL, English Skills for Life! And I liked the people I met, the centre where I went, Park Lane College, is far more than a College, it is a social centre. The students, most of them middle-eastern, ate breakfast together then spent the rest of the day hanging out with each other. The work of the teachers was not just teaching, but integration. Even though most of the students were from the Middle East, we got to know the cultures of other students too, Poles, Czechs, Spaniards, Italians - my experience of Leeds could not have been better.

I leave the cafe and set off to lead my writing workshop at the old people's home in Headingley. Everyone likes to write about their experiences, their thoughts. But few people know how to write, few have the technique.

I suggest a theme. It's an advanced class, so I presume they are up to writing about concepts, not just the usual banalities of family visits and childhood memories. I come up with Coincidence and ask them if they believe everything has a reason. The majority say yes, god determines everything. But one of them, and old guy with onset Alzheimers who spends his day in the gardens, surprises me. He tells us he does not believe in gods but, for him, the universe obeys some mathematical formula which we don't understand. He says it wouldn't surprise him to see a dinosaur in the park, because potentially anything is possible. He tells us that life has treated him badly and the only thing he asks for is that it treats his only son better. So far it has turned out that way, his son is a successful DJ. So I change the theme of the week and ask them to write a story about someone they know whose live has changed direction when they least expected it. This causes a few murmurs and grumbles as I leave, and that's the class done for another week.

Headingley Lane envelopes me in a grey blanket of misery. It is nearly midday and my stomach is demanding to be fed. I fancy Thai, so pop into the Bangkok cafe for spicy noodles. I always have the noodles, even though they are never quite hot enough.

3.

To really dedicate yourself to something you have to pay a high price. I live isolated in my own world. Neither polygamous nor monogamous, I don't need women around me. From time to time I resort to masturbation and occasionally, during moments of more relaxed spirituality, I've paid for the company of a young lady. But the bad side of paying to cum, is that afterwards it seems as though you have achieved nothing. Because of this I try and maintain a distance from bodily desires. The spicy noodles are always a mistake, they don't agree with me, so I go home for bicarbonate of soda and lie down for a while. The good thing about being a writer is the hours. I prefer to work at night.

At five thirty I have one of the most important appointments of my life, my world will stop and everything will revolve around my novel, my personal success. I will detach myself from any community spirit and be entirely selfish. I know that's a not good thing but I want it, I deserve it, all I have now is indigestion from the noodles, I look in the cupboard for anti-acids.

Capsules. The universe is made of capsules that form one around the other and so on and so on ad infinitum. My consciousness is a little capsule inside many others: LS6, Leeds, Yorkshire, England, Europe, The World, the Solar System ... but not only this, the capsules that don't contain each other co-exist tangentially, but can partially incorporate each other like Venn diagrams. In mine, that is in LS6, I can see myself within other capsules, like Benjamin's when I involve myself in his problems, form part of his life story, his thoughts, his desires. This is why the ego is ridiculous because it is no more than one capsule lost among thousands, millions more. Everything is related to everything else to articulate the whole, like the nervous system which uses all its transmitters interacting to define the behaviour of an individual. The world is complex and difficult to think about, but that's exactly what I like doing the most.

I set off walking towards the city centre where, in one of the office blocks, the editor waits for me. He is called Richardson, I call him The Editor, but our relationship is no less commercial than the ones I have with the checkout girl in the Co-op or the cashier in Bank of Scotland. Editors know that for most people, publishing a book is the high point of their life, so these publishers of last resort, whose only interest is money not quality, call all the shots and have complete control their over self-funded authors. It is only the pride of most writers that prevents self-publishing dominating the market.

I ring the doorbell, clear my throat, run my fingers through my hair and push the door open. In the lift I clear my throat again and when the door opens a fat guy with a shiny black wig and no moustache greets me with his hand held out. I squeeze his hand, look into his eyes, see his cufflinks reflected in his chin. He leads me inside with a typical British off-handedness, I doubt that even JK Rowling would be received with any more enthusiasm. He is thinking, This one wants to sell me something.

'You know Mr Ramtin, I also worked as a ghost writer for some time,' he says leaning back in his seat, 'It is a good way to learn, besides being well paid. But you have to go little by little, Ramtin, you can't go from black to white like Michael Jackson, if you know what I mean?'

'Sure I understand, you deal in numbers and I with letters, but I understand.'

'This is a business Mr Ramtin, we're no cultural not-for-profit. We can't lose money -' he says as the phone rings - 'I am sorry, I need to take this call. I won't be a minute.'

A minute becomes five. The editor repeats the same phrases over and over. The telling-off that the other person is receiving is not at all pleasant. My editor's shiny cuff links and dry, aggressive tone make it clear that he is the boss. Just when he seems about to hang up, the telling off picks up again and the dressing down continues. I occupy myself with my thoughts, making plans and calculations.

'I understand what you are saying,' I say when he has hung up. 'This is why I have not come here thinking you would publish me and cover all of the costs.'

'Of course,' he interrupts, 'I am sure you understand that I can't invest in a Kurdish author with no track record, selling an Iranian refugee in England would make paupers of us all.'

'I don't see why, look at Azar Nifisi.'

'But she's different, she writes the kind of memoirs that our very popular in this country. Your book is a philosophical treatise in the form of a novel, Mr Ramtin, we could not sell more than two dozen copies.'

His secretary comes in and interrupts our conversation. She asks the editor to step out to deal with a distributor wanting to talk to him urgently. He excuses himself and I prepare to be kept hanging about for another ten to fifteen minutes. I mentally rehearse my alternative proposal.

4.

Twenty minutes. His twenty minute chat with the distributor, for me becomes twenty minutes of increasing anger and frustration. I feel like strangling this dickhead, but to reject all my years of work is a pleasure that this editor doesn't deserve. When he comes back I paste on a smile and once again, accept his apologies.

'What a day.' He sighs, 'Well, as I was saying, I can't offer you more than the self-financing option.'

'Yes, that's what you were saying, but I'd like to propose an alternative.'

'Go ahead.' He says, convinced he won't be accepting it.

'I guarantee that the first thousand copies will sell.

Between my contacts in bookshops, the writing classes that I give and the reading clubs, I could sell a thousand no problem. If, for some reason, I don't sell that many I'll pay you back the difference after six months.'

'Even if you paid me and I kept all the profits, I would still lose money. Business is about investment and I am looking to double my money at least. Dead money deteriorates, if money isn't working its value can only decrease. That's the first rule of economics, Mr Ramtin. I am afraid that I can really only offer you self-financing.'

'OK, I came prepared to accept that, I knew you wouldn't negotiate and I'd have to risk my own money. That's the way of the West, that's the way it goes.'

'Come on, Mr Ramtin, stop beating about the bush.'

'You would prefer me to be direct? You surprise me, are you sure you are really English?'

His cynical smile invites me to continue.

'As I was saying, I'd like you to commit to financing my second book if the first one is successful.'

'And how would you define success?'

'Well, just setting up a press, or any business could be seen as success, a commercial success if it pays dividends. However, I am not looking for the same success as you. To paraphrase Victor Hugo, success is an ugly thing, men are deceived by its false resemblance to merit.'

'And you think your work has merit?'

'Yes.'

'Good. And what exactly is this book you have in mind?'

'Like I said before, the West is the West. Here everything works, but no one explains how it works, nobody examines the experience. So everything is uncertain, man has abandoned himself to chance, intent only on survival. You live in the shallows, where passion rules. All of which makes here the perfect place to implement The Plan.'

'What plan?'

'The plan of false liberty. It relies on the illusion that we think we are free and, compared to other places on earth, it seems we are. But in reality, we are more controlled than anywhere else because in the West people think so little. You think sideways, without trying to understand, without experimenting. Look around you, every step we take is recorded by CCTV, our personal data, every part of our lives is recorded by the internet, stored in databases, our telephones are being rung incessantly by machines trying to sell us things, salesmen knock down our doors. We are ripe for mind control, reverted to primitive beings, consumers ready for manipulation, adverts saturating our brains. In the end we all fall. The Plan lets a handful of people use the perfect weapon - information technology - to control the world through our finances. But naked greed has opened up a crack in the system and set off the alarms, the liars are against the ropes. People are asking for nationalisations and protectionism, asking for change, shouting the buzzwords of Obama, Yes, we can win. Yes, we are able to change the world because we realise we have been tricked. But because Obama wants to stay in power he too is obliged to lie. He says he is going to reform the system, intervene more, but this can only be done through regulation, which the vested interests will resist, big money will do for him, money is god. The crisis exploded the modern world and those of us who have survived must spread the truths we have discovered. Our mission as citizens should be to make the whole world know that there is this plan that governs everything. It is already too late to stop it, so the least that we can do is try to control it democratically.'

'Sorry, I'm losing you. You're talking about a western plan, but you know that world trade is dominated by China, they're partly to blame for the collapse of the system.'

'They are cleverer than the Americans. They have a much older culture. They co-exist with nature in a much more organic, less demanding way than those wasteful Americans. My theory is, it's all to do with religion. The Plan can only take root in the West where people are blind to their own ignorance. Christianity saying go forth and multiply only creates more herds of mindless people who fight each other for resources and get desperate. Those who are desperate are capable of believing anything. Christianity, like the whole of western philosophy, asks transcendental questions but doesn't answer them. Buddhism however, searches for experience, uses the real world.'

'Now you've completely lost me.'

'Praying on your knees in church is an empty spiritual experience. The faithful neither know for what or to whom they are praying, they don't know how to communicate with the divine and are incapable of feeling it, trapped in their religion. Yoga, on the other hand, is a spiritual exercise that makes god something more than an icon with a beard and a halo on his head. Yoga is a means of knowing and understanding instead of just believing. Mysticism is what's left when there is no more science.'

'Mm, if you are as serious as you seem to be, how are you

going to convey all this?'

'Well, you see-'

The telephone again! Now I know why business men have no friends, just social lives consisting only of people like them.

5.

Much to my surprise, Richardson shouts that he is busy and hangs up. My ideas have finally caught his attention.

'Go on, Ramtin, tell me how you plan to write this.'

'If we agree that the basis of everything is an eternal circle without beginning or end, and that everything repeats cyclically, the novel could be a tangle of interrelations in which everyone depends on everyone else. Like our organism, like in nature, like the economic and financial systems. This is the world today, the same as it was yesterday.

'You leave me speechless.'

'Does that mean you accept?'

'OK, Ramtin. Here's the deal. Finance the first book

yourself and if sales break even, I will cover the costs of this other book. Does it have a title?'

'No, I haven't written it yet. At the moment it is all in this yellow notebook.'

'Then take care. Don't lose it.'

'I am thinking of LS6.'

'Something so complex and you are going to call it after a stinking suburb of Leeds.'

'LS6 could refer to an engine produced by General Motors, or a kind of ultra-light glider, a type of LSD, it could stand for anything. LS6 is its own world, a world that happens every day, a world in itself with everything that occurs in it. That's why, with it being something so complex, I can use any title I want.'

The editor eased his large body out of his chair and reached a hand towards me.

'Very well, Mr Ramtin, my congratulations. I'll be in touch soon about the contract and let you know what the costs will be. If you have any questions don't hesitate to call me.'

'Agreed, thank you for hearing me out.'

'You're welcome, Mr Ramtin. So, what are you off to do now?'

'Now? Nothing. It's late. I don't think I'll do anything.'

'One of the calls that interrupted us was my wife, letting me know our evening at this Thatcher play at Playhouse is off. My youngest has a fever. If it was left to me, we'd just give her Calpol and go, but you know, it's the women who call the shots in the end! So I've two tickets going spare, do you want them?'

After winning over Richardson I had thought my day was

complete, but I do love the theatre and I've been wanting to see The Death of Margaret Thatcher. The Playhouse is only a mile from here. I have time to walk. I like walking. Walking is the best way of thinking. The problem with western intellectualism is the sofa. Thinkers write from the bubble of their seats, no experimentation, no using their brain at the same time as their muscles. Thinking stimulated by motion increases the power of the mind. My imagination will fill the pages of my novel while I walk. An interesting phrase occurs to me, I stop and write it down. I slip my yellow notebook back in my pocket and carry on walking with a light step.

The sky seems finally to have made a truce with the first day of spring, and the pavements on the way to the West Yorkshire Playhouse are full of life: a stall of second hand clothes, a hot dog stand, a man selling balloons, couples arm in arm, people who have just left work, even a few Japanese tourists with their cameras. The show is about to begin, the last of the audience are going in, I join the back of the queue. In the auditorium the lights have already gone down and the usher, a tall guy with a beard shows me to my seat in the front row. He points with his torch and says,

'Enjoy the show!'

Leo Carragher. Leeds. April 2009.

Mario Crespo was born in Zamora, Spain in 1979. He studied the History of Art and Librarianship at the University of Salmanca and is the Director of short films 'Untitled' and 'Death'. LS6 was first published in Spanish in 2010 and it was chosen to represent Spain at the Festival du Premier Roman de Chambéry , "Cuento kilómetros" (2011), "Biblioteca Nacional" (2012) and "La 4ª" (2014). Mario currently lives in Madrid.

Sally Ashton grew up in Yorkshire and from the age of sixteen has been involved in the Writing Squad (an Arts Council initiative for young Northern writers). She studied Creative Writing at the University of Warwick and has also completed a Masters in Translation and Interpreting at the University of Westminster. In amongst her degrees she has travelled extensively and has also spent time working in France, Canada, Spain and Austria. She currently lives in Berlin, working as a translator. In her spare time she loves playing sport, reading and drinking coffee.

Sally Ashton's first novel, Controller, was shortlisted for the Route Young Author award and the Sabotage Review's Best Novella award. It is out now, published by Dead Ink Books.

Steve Dearden's short stories have been published in Single Skin (Smith Doorstop) and in magazines in the UK, Finland and Australia. He is also a producer and the founding Director of The Writing Squad, the development programme for young writers in the north of England. Before that he was Director of the Ilkley Literature Festival and the National Association for Literature Development and Literature Officer for Yorkshire Arts. He has recently returned home to Manchester. www.stevedearden.com